Leaving Point

Leaving Point

BETTY VANDER ELS

Farrar Straus Giroux

New York

Special thanks to Emma Brodbeck and to my father
for generously sharing their experiences,
and to Margaret Ferguson, my editor

For my parents, Signe, Sam and Gerry Jeffery,
and for my sister and brothers, Barb, Bob and John,
with love and respect

Leaving Point

ONE

The strangest year in my life began with the Christmas
holiday of 1950, just after I turned fourteen. Looking at
that time is like squinting through the wrong end of a
telescope: the figures are small and far away; they move
in a troubled setting halfway round the world, at a time
when ancient past and modern present heaved in topsy-
turvydom. As I tossed like a cork with the rest of the
flotsam and jetsam of that storm, I gained my first understanding of the Chinese Communist Revolution.

For the past three years, I had been living at a boarding
school for missionary children in the hill country of east-
ern China with my two younger brothers, Simeon and
Benjamin. Our parents had sent Miss Lin to escort us
west to Chengtu, where they had been running a mission
station for eight months.

We were traveling by bus, on the final lap of our journey, when the motor stopped. The children rubbed peep-
holes in the fog on the windows, as they had done every
time the bus stopped; then, when nothing more happened, they lost interest and let the holes fog over. At
this rate, I thought, the holiday will be over before we
even reach Chengtu.

"Are they all right, Ruth?" From her seat behind the

driver, Miss Lin's anxious voice repeated the question she'd asked so many times during the long trip. "Are they all there?"

Dutifully I stood up in my place toward the back and counted the younger children sitting among the Chinese soldiers in the rattletrap, greenish-gray bus. "Does she think they'll fall through the floor or something?" I whispered to Simeon, who was sitting next to me, but he just shrugged. I bit my lip, glanced away from him, and nodded to Miss Lin.

"Are they?" she asked again.

"Of course," I answered irritably. "There are still eleven of them." Poor Miss Lin gave an apologetic smile, and I was sorry for my rudeness. "Yes, they're all right," I said more gently to the tiny Chinese Bible teacher. I sat back down; between us, the other children were squashed against the windows here and there. Soldiers filled the rest of the bus, many standing in the aisle.

The engine coughed, spluttered, and started. We jounced on over the dirt road through the rain. In the front seats, half a dozen soldiers laughed and shouted more and more noisily. One of them held a piece of sugarcane over his head while the others reached for it. I couldn't tell whether it was a game or a dispute.

About an hour later, the bus gave a tremendous lurch and stopped again. I wiped the fog off the window and tried to see through the rain. "The city gates!" I exclaimed. "We must be nearly there! I don't believe it."

"Where do you see the gates?" Simeon asked.

"Where?" The other children grimaced and squinted, trying to see.

"Over there," I said. "Where the road curves."

Our long journey was almost over. It was a trip that should have taken as little as four or five days, but had already stretched into three harassing weeks. During those early chaotic years of the revolution, rules varied from day to day and from city to city. We didn't know until we reached each place which officers had to be notified, or what exactly they might want. Transportation, erratic at best, was even more unpredictable than usual. We didn't know, until the boat, train, or bus actually arrived and we saw it, whether there would be one; and then we didn't know if it would leave, until we boarded and felt it moving.

Nervously Miss Lin stood up, twisting and turning to count us once more. I was thoroughly tired of her anxiety, though I understood it. As the eldest, I had been responsible for the twelve of us whenever she went off to arrange for tickets and passes in each city we had traveled through. I was glad the other children would be continuing on to their parents' nearby villages after we got to Chengtu.

The driver and the sugarcane soldiers got into an excited argument, jumped off the bus, and disappeared. The rain pounded on the bus roof. The remaining soldiers drowsed and the children fidgeted. "We're so near!" I exclaimed to Simeon. "Why do we have to break down now!"

He smiled to himself, completely absorbed in his own dreams.

Well, it can't be too much longer before we really see Mum and Dad, I thought; the city gates are right there down the road. Happily, I imagined my parents, whom I hadn't seen for three years. Dad was a big man, pretty stern, but we knew he cared; and he was always in control of the situation, not like poor Miss Lin. Mum was warm and attentive, ready to stop and listen to us any time. They were wonderful. In a few more hours, there'd be just our family and maybe two or three other missionaries. We'd go for walks and investigate this new city; we'd meet some of the Chinese friends they'd described in letters to us. I hoped there would be a fireplace and a sofa in their new home, where we could all sit together and chat or play board games.

The driver and the sugarcane soldiers returned, sopping wet and smiling. The bus shuddered, filled with fumes from the engine, and pitched forward again. At last, we passed through the gates of the city.

Miss Lin left us in a room at the police station, which was always our first stopping point. "Keep the children quiet," she told me, glancing apprehensively at the two policemen sent to watch us. "I will go and find what I must do."

"Aren't you going to take us to Mummy and Daddy?" my younger brother, Benjamin, burst out.

Miss Lin fidgeted with her satchel of papers. "I will try to contact them," she said, and left, murmuring to herself.

We huddled uncertainly in the corner of the bleak room. Some of the little ones picked at their coat buttons, nearly twisting them off; a couple of others snickered nervously behind their hands, and several kept poking me and whispering, "When do we get to see our mums and dads?"

"Soon, I hope. Soon," I whispered back.

We were dwarfed by two ubiquitous portraits hanging

high on the wall. Chairman Mao Tse-tung stared benignly over our heads at the closed door at the far end of the room. Stalin's grim brown eyes glared down on us all. I had learned to hate his face. It epitomized for me the suspicion of all the officials we had met on our journey. But that face also made me feel guilty when any of the kids misbehaved, since I was responsible for them, and worried what would happen if they got into trouble.

Particularly Benjamin, I thought, as I glanced first at my irrepressible brother, then at the forbidding face. I pushed from the back of the huddle and reached across the pile of suitcases to try and catch him. He was balanced on the rung of a chair, clearly preparing to sit on top of the desk. "You little silly!" I whispered.

As I grabbed Benjamin's collar, the button of my old blue coat sleeve caught in his hair. "Hey! Stop that!" he said. Carefully, I untangled his curl and started to pull him toward me.

"Leave him! Leave him!" the two short Chinese police officers chorused from the other side of the desk. They nudged each other, tittered, and settled that rascal into the large official black chair. The top of his curly head reached the middle of its back.

Impishly, Benjamin glanced into the men's faces, then clapped to get the other children's attention. "Simeon, here!" he commanded his older brother in Chinese, for the benefit of the men. We used both English and Chinese; some of the littlest ones used them together without realizing it. Benjamin slapped a place on the desk and looked up.

The two men nodded vigorously; their hair flipflopped on their foreheads. Simeon passed me a martyred look, and leaned uncomfortably against the desk. He could see that the officers expected him to cooperate with Benjamin.

Pleased with his success, Benjamin clapped again and pointed. "Trevor, here! Alexandra, here! James, Ivan, Danny, here!" Several smaller children scrambled over. "Althea–Antonia, here!" They were twin girls who acted so much like an image and its reflection that they were treated as one person and their names said in one breath. They had short fair hair and large blue eyes. Giggling and bumping against the men, they squeezed into place.

The men bent double with silent laughter.

"These Chengtu police are nice!" Benjamin announced. "Not like some of those horrid ones in the other cities."

I leaned apprehensively toward him. "Better be careful. Maybe it's a trick," I whispered.

"Don't worry," he assured me airily. "Police usually like me." He slapped another spot on the desk. "Sylvia, here!" A very small girl with frightened gray eyes picked her way toward him. She had spent most of the journey whimpering with fear.

The door at the far end of the room opened; the two short policemen jerked to attention. Benjamin laughed.

"Shut up!" Simeon hissed sourly and stood up straight. But Benjamin just smirked, leaned forward, and deliberately put his elbows up on the edge of the desk. I couldn't think how to control him.

"Come here," I whispered to the rest. They shuffled back into the corner against me.

Three new officers marched in, scowling. One wore thick glasses and had a mole on his neck just above his stiff, revolutionary-jacket collar. Behind these three came a pretty, slender police girl, her black hair tied in a red scarf and covered with a cap.

Then I caught my breath, torn by the first sight of my father. He walked in, slightly stooped, as if he'd grown old and shorter. He wore dusty bicycle clips around his gray trouser cuffs, and his suit jacket seemed thin for the weather. He gave us an eager, guarded smile.

"Daddy!" Benjamin shouted, and slid off the chair. But Dad's face turned strangely sober and he made no move toward us. "What's the matter, Daddy?" Benjamin asked, completely baffled.

"Quiet!" one of the new officers commanded. "Stay still! This is the police office of the People's Republic of China! Have you no respect?"

My little brother put both hands on the corner of the desk and looked at Dad, but Dad said nothing. Then Benjamin squinted at the two short policemen, whose eyes had shifted to a fly buzzing in front of them.

"Take your hands from that desk!" one of the new officers ordered Benjamin. "Stand straight!" The man gestured toward the rest of us. I put an arm around Sylvia. "Their escort? Their papers?" Even Benjamin frowned and stood straight as a stick.

Just then Miss Lin, in her quilted blue ankle-length gown and half-fingered knitted gloves, bustled in, chattering under her breath. "I am their escort," she announced in a high, jittery voice. "I brought them from their school in Kuling." She held up a sheaf of official papers to the officer. He took them, strode to the desk, and shooed Benjamin back into the corner with the rest of us.

9

Then he sat down, frowning, spread the papers methodically in front of him, rearranged them a couple of times, and began to read very carefully. His frown deepened as if something displeased him, and my heart sank. "How long are they to visit?" he snapped.

"Two weeks," Dad replied meekly.

"You are sure?"

Dad glanced at the papers in surprise, then back at the man. "The return date should be there," he said uncertainly, and moved to where he could read over the man's shoulder.

The officer ran a chipped fingernail down the lines of elegantly written characters while Dad followed.

"There." Dad touched the document. "I think that's the date."

"It is smudged. It has been tampered with," the man scolded. "Bring them here for permission to leave before you try to buy tickets back to their school. Do you understand?"

"Yes. But you will allow them back, won't you?" Dad asked. In my parents' missionary society, our education was considered of primary importance. Keeping us with them but without a formal education was a second choice, in spite of the unsettled times.

"There is no set date. Come back in two weeks. Then we will see. Write a report of their journey. Bring it to me tomorrow. Go!"

Dad stood for a minute, stunned. He must have known it was impossible to make definite plans, but I guess he hadn't expected this particular problem. However, he knew better than to ask questions.

"Go!" the officer commanded.

TWO

Dad wasted no more time trying to clarify our papers while all of us were at the police station. "Come on, kiddies," he said. "Bring your suitcases."

I picked up my old brown one with the rope handle. "Is your compound far from here?"

"Not too far. I took so long because we had no idea when you'd arrive and I was out when the call came," Dad said. "Come on," he repeated to the others.

"Do we get to see our mums and dads now?" Trevor asked eagerly, and shoved his glasses up his stubby nose.

"What did that man say?" Benjamin wanted to know.

"Quiet! Go in order!" The officer's voice smothered the noisy excitement. We looked in fright at the man, knowing it wouldn't take much to provoke new reprimands and more delays, and formed a line behind Dad. I knew I wouldn't feel safe until we had walked through the gates of the mission compound.

Outside the police station, seven coolies hunkered beside their rickshaws. Miss Lin stepped into one. "We will meet this evening," she told Dad. Her carrier snorted to clear his nose, and spat in the street, as he stood to pull her in his carefully repaired rickshaw.

Dad put his hands together, palm to palm, and bowed

in a gesture of deep gratitude. Then he turned to us and said, "Hop in!" with a cheerfulness I knew was put on. He rubbed his chin in a way he used to do when he was uneasy. "Simeon and Ruth, you'd best each take a little one, to balance things a bit." He glanced uncomfortably at a cluster of soldiers eyeing us with obvious suspicion.

"I'll take Danny," Simeon quickly said.

"Trevor and me can go together, can't we?" Benjamin asked argumentatively.

"No," Dad told him in a voice Benjamin recognized and obeyed. "You'll go with Ruth." For a moment he sounded more like his old self.

Benjamin pursed his lips, glowered at me, and deliberately tossed his suitcase onto the floor of the rickshaw near my toe. I couldn't help but chuckle. "Silly old thing." He grinned and climbed in next to me.

Dad, pedaling his black Philips bicycle, led the column, with two of us in each rickshaw. Our breath rose like vague banners in the chilly air.

We rode through nearly empty streets lined with small wooden houses and shops set one right next to the other. A few old women sat on stools outside their shops coolly watching us. A man, who looked like an elderly scholar, lowered his head, took off his glasses, and started polishing them with the sleeve of his gown. A group of children playing at the side of a street snickered and pointed. "Foreign spies! American robbers!" they shouted enthusiastically. One boy snarled and threw pebbles.

I shrank down in my seat. I remembered how different it was several years earlier during the Second World War in Loshan, the town where our school had been. Then we were the "good Americans." People wanted to touch our clothes, and laughed at our big noses and blue eyes, but all with good-humored curiosity. On this journey, we had met few people like that.

At one corner, a column of about twenty women appeared, carrying baskets of stones on shoulder yokes. "What are they doing?" Benjamin asked.

"Don't point," I whispered. Our rickshaw jolted into a hole and then stopped as we waited for the women to pass. I fell against Benjamin and grabbed his hand. "Fixing roads, Miss Lin said. I saw several groups at the river as we came into the city."

The last woman trotted by. I looked at Dad, leaning slightly against his bicycle. Not one person so far had called out in friendly greeting; not even a child had called, "Mr. Tan!" using his Chinese name, as they had when I was a little girl.

I realized I was still holding Benjamin's hand, as he craned curiously around after the disappearing crew of stone carriers. We plunged forward again over the cobblestones until we reached the middle of a short block, Paper Lantern Street, where we stopped at a solid black wooden gate set in an eight-foot wall. Dad paid the rickshaw carriers, who jogged away to look for more work. Then he banged on the gate, shouting, "Kai mun! Kai mun!"—"Open the gate!"

Four soldiers marched past and stopped on the corner to watch us. We waited in a fidgeting group.

Simeon stood behind Dad, twisting from side to side. "Dad, what's that?" he asked, pointing to a large sheet of rice paper pasted on the wall of the compound.

Dad turned and frowned. "A list of people who live on this street," he explained.

Simeon touched the red circle around one name. "What's this mean?"

Dad ignored the question and turned back to the gate. "Where's that gatekeeper?" he wondered aloud and shouted again. "Kai mun! Kai mun!"

Simeon looked curiously at him and took his finger from the red circle.

The gate opened.

My heart sank. A miserable recollection washed over me of saying goodbye to my parents three years ago. The more I responded now to their affection, the harder it would be to harness those feelings when it was time to say goodbye again. I was frustrated and confused. "I'm afraid," I whispered to Simeon.

"Afraid!" he echoed, as if he couldn't believe what he was hearing. "Whatever for?"

I shrugged my shoulders, not knowing how to explain.

"Up, little girl. Up, little boy," the smiling gatekeeper sang out as he lifted the smallest children over the eighteen-inch threshold. When everyone was inside, he slid the big wooden bolt back into place, turned, and stood with his hands on his hips, nodding happily as the children hurried toward the house.

A path led between flanking gardens, empty now because it was winter, to the mission home: a large, rambling, two-story building. The jutting rooms, occasional skylights, and verandas had an intriguingly unplanned appearance. To the left was a wide lawn, and to the right a row of leafless trees. An eight-foot wall surrounded everything, including sheds and a bamboo grove with a small building behind it.

Dad and I were at the end of the line. I glanced at

14

him. He smiled and pushed his bike slowly forward. "You've had your hands full, haven't you?"

"I sure have!" I burst out. "Three weeks of that lot!" I bit my lip, knowing I shouldn't complain. But I was very relieved to be rid of the responsibility.

"You've a good head on your shoulders, Ruth. Miss Lin told me how helpful you've been." I was so unaccustomed to praise that I didn't know what to say.

A door slammed erratically as adults crowded out of the mission home.

"Trevor!"

"You've grown so!"

"Mummy!"

"Daddy!"

". . . so glad you're safely here!"

". . . three weeks getting here."

"Thank God!"

I couldn't imagine why the parents hadn't sent someone to escort their children on, instead of all coming to Chengtu. "Why are they all here?" I asked, gesturing toward the crowd.

"They're staying," Dad explained.

"Till tomorrow?"

"No," he said. "For the whole holiday."

"The whole holiday!" I was appalled. "What do you mean?"

"It's taken so long to get you all here nobody wanted to risk more delays." He turned toward the bike shed.

I stood absolutely still, then closed my eyes for a minute, trying to wipe out what was happening in front of me.

"Mummy! I'm here!" Benjamin yelled, and barged

through the others up to the veranda, almost colliding with Mum as she came out the door. "Mummy! Mummy!" he bellowed, as he threw himself at her and held her in the vise of his arms.

Beside me, Simeon sighed, waiting for Mum to raise her head and notice him. "Plaguey little squirt," he muttered.

My fear and confusion grew. "I'm just as glad—" I started, then realized Simeon didn't share my relief at the delay. I felt as if I was about to step onto a flimsy suspension bridge which might not hold. Benjamin was cute and little; I felt big and awkward in comparison, and because so much time had passed, uncertain what my mother might think of me.

At last, Mum reached behind her back with both her hands and unlocked Benjamin's. He grinned up at her and ran off. Quickly she hurried down the edge of the path, with her warm, familiar smile. "Ruth! Simeon!" she said, and put her arms around the two of us. It was the most wonderful feeling in the world. All of my fears vanished—I knew I was home.

三

THREE

"Where will everyone fit?" I asked Mum as the three of us walked up the path.

She gave a brief laugh. "Everything's been turned into bedrooms. No more ironing room, mending room, clothes-drying room. We've had to scour the city for beds and folks brought their own bedding. One family to a room." She gave us each a pat. "But you're here and that's the main thing."

Later that afternoon, we were finally alone in our bed-room. I sat on the edge of my bed, not knowing what to say. Simeon, whose bed was pushed against the wall, leaned back with a half-smile on his face. And from the middle of his bed, Benjamin entertained us with a de-tailed account of his cleverness at the police station. Mum and Dad sat side by side on theirs, listening, but they both looked faintly worried, or preoccupied—I couldn't tell which.

"I told all those—"

Benjamin was interrupted by a short, elderly mission-ary lady in a paisley shawl who stood at the open door. She leaned in. "So sorry to trouble you, but can you find me a jug for drinking water, Mrs. Thompson?" she asked. "Must have my six glasses a day, you know."

Immediately Mum got up and went with her. A look of disappointment crossed Simeon's face. "Silly old twit," I muttered to him. "Why doesn't she just look for a jug herself." Fortunately, Benjamin was already talking again, so Dad didn't hear my rude comment.

Before long, the twins' mother poked her head around the door. "Oh, I'm so glad to have found you, Mr. Thompson. Can you come? There's something not quite right with the little girls' passports." Dad got up and followed her out.

Benjamin looked mildly surprised. "Oh, well, if they're gone I might as well have a look around." He bounced off his bed and out the door.

I stared at the empty doorway. "I wonder if this is how it's going to be the whole time?" I complained, remembering my happy imaginings before the bus reached Chengtu.

Simeon hunched forward on his bed and stared down at his hands, too absorbed in his own disappointment to reply.

"I guess I'll get my suitcase," I muttered. "Do you want to get yours?" I waited. "Do you?" I asked impatiently.

Slowly he shook his head, and went on staring at his thumbs, twisting them over and over in his lap.

Supper that night was crowded and full of interrupted conversations and laughter. Dad had to leave before we were finished, to work with Miss Lin on the report for the police. The meal went on so long a couple of the smallest children fell asleep, their heads resting against the edge of the table.

When everyone was finally finished, Mum cleaned and

wiped down the huge table, with sporadic help from one or two other adults. I wandered aimlessly about, coming into the dining room at intervals to see if she was finished. Simeon leaned against the wall, content just to be near her. During one of my passes through the room, she looked at her watch. "Benjamin!" she exclaimed as he ducked briefly in the doorway. "Go upstairs! Now! Get ready for bed. I'll be along in a while to say prayers with you. It's way past your bedtime."

He trotted to the front hall and stopped there with his back to the main door. On his right was the narrow hall to Dad's study. The sound of his voice and Miss Lin's came faintly through the door. Benjamin glanced to his left at a few single missionaries sitting in the enormous living room, then looked straight ahead up the short flight of wooden stairs to the landing, where they divided. "Botheration!" he muttered as he bounded up.

"Ayah. Ayah." Mum sighed.

Simeon and I smiled hearing the expression, because we remembered her using it when she was bothered. "What's the matter?" I asked.

"The table's pulled all the way out," she said, "but it was such a squeeze at supper, I think we'll have to eat in shifts." She started setting out teaspoons and bone-handled knives for breakfast.

"How does this place work, anyhow?" I asked.

"Twenty-two, twenty-three," she murmured, and looked up. "What did you say?" I repeated my question. "Dad does all the bookkeeping and transportation and so on, and I manage the house. Usually it's just for ten or twelve people staying less than a week. But now there must be about thirty of us!" She picked up some more

19

spoons. "We came right after Benjamin went to school, about eight months ago. With so many missionaries leaving the country, it's hard to find people to run this network of stations the mission has."

"Will everyone really have to stay for the whole holiday? Dad made it sound like—" I began.

"Don't even think it!" Mum exclaimed. "Some of them are single folk who arrived last week and are supposed to be going on any day now. Only the parents will stay until all of you go back to school."

I watched her busy hands, as I tried to get my bearings for this strange, bittersweet homecoming. It looked as though Mum and Dad were going to be at everyone's beck and call the whole time. And the fact that they didn't know the day of our arrival bothered me unreasonably. "Did you really not even know when we were coming?" I asked.

Mum chuckled and went on setting the table. "Not until the police telephoned, and then the line crackled so badly we didn't know what they were talking about. I still can't believe you're here; all those days of not knowing where you'd gotten to. We thought we had everything so carefully worked out to get you here in just a few days. But that doesn't seem to make much difference anymore." Mum patted my shoulder, then pulled open a drawer for another napkin.

Simeon asked, "Is Dad going to be this busy the whole time?"

"Lately he has been, with all the toing and froing for police permission for every blessed thing we do." She sighed. "Nobody else knows local rules and regulations like he does. And we didn't expect all the families were going to have to come here until the last minute."

"Phew, I'm tired." Simeon yawned hugely.

"So am I," I added.

"Why don't you both go on up. Make sure Benjamin remembers he's supposed to be getting to bed." Mum started counting out porridge bowls.

We went toward the stairs. "This is going to be an off-the-map holiday, that's for sure," I grumbled.

"Whatever do you mean?" Simeon asked.

"Nothing's turning out like I expected," I said resentfully.

"Yes. But we're *home*!" He gave a happy sigh.

"I suppose." I pushed open the bedroom door. "Where *is* that little demon?" I wondered.

"Can't you just forget about him?" Simeon asked.

Benjamin's footsteps clumped up the stairs. I met him at the door. "Where have you been?"

"Meeting some Goodnight Ladies by mistake," he informed me.

"You what?" I peered uneasily down the long hall, feebly lit by one bulb hanging from the ceiling, but it was empty.

He pointed to the other side of the house. "The other hall," he explained. "I went there by mistake, and I couldn't remember our door, so I started at the beginning."

"Who was in that room?" I asked in alarm, thinking of some of the stern faces at supper.

He laughed. "It was dark. There was just giggles."

"Who?"

"Althea–Antonia and their sisters. Alexandra said I

couldn't sleep in their mum and dad's bed." He laughed. "And of course Aileen was grumpy."

"Where else did you go?"

"To a room that smelled like a coffin."

"What do you mean?" I asked.

"You know, that smell when the carpenters are shaving coffin planks on the street."

"Camphor. Who was in there?"

He put on his monkey grin. "The Goodnight Ladies. And one of them said, 'Saints alive, sweet St. Ive! I thought it was the police again.' She was wearing a shawl and reading her Chinese Bible. And one of them was packing things into a suitcase. And the other one looked like a pillow and—"

"Benjamin, that's rude."

"Well, she did," he went on, "because of her quilted gown. She asked me what I thought I was doing."

"What did you say?" I asked suspiciously.

"I said I was looking for my room," he explained innocently, "because I was. And she said, 'This is *not* your room,' which I could see easy enough. So I said, 'No. I guess it isn't. Good night, ladies, I'm going to leave you.' Just like Daddy used to say when he was being funny!" he finished triumphantly. "So that's why they're Goodnight Ladies!"

"Oh, Benjamin!" I sighed and tried not to smile. "I hope that was all."

"Then I went to the end of the hall, and there's only the veranda, so I came back and tried the other stairs and here I am!"

Simeon gave a disgusted sniff, finished buttoning his pajamas, and slid into bed.

"Hurry up. Get ready now," I told Benjamin. "I want to turn out the light."

"Why don't you put on your pajamas," he challenged.

"I will, but under the covers," I answered self-consciously. "Now get in."

FOUR

Four days later, I still felt confused and was beginning to grow angry. The only time we had with Mum and Dad was snatched time. After breakfast, I told Mum, "We *did* bring Christmas presents."

She stacked a pile of dirty porridge bowls. "I wonder if those single ladies will go today," she said to herself. "What did you say, Ruth?"

I repeated my almost accusing comment.

"Oh, Ruth, I'm sorry. I had hoped things would quiet down a bit so we could celebrate. But—" She made a second stack of bowls. "Find Simeon and Benjamin and go to the bedroom. I'll be along as soon as I can. And tell Dad, too."

The boys and I waited, Benjamin bouncing on and off the beds, Simeon lolling against the wall. "I couldn't find Dad," I told Mum when she arrived.

She frowned. "Oh, I forgot. He went off to see about those ladies' exit visas."

"What're exit visas?"

"They're papers for leaving. But we better go ahead without Dad, I don't know when he'll get home." She bent to pull something out from under their bed. "This is for you, Ruth." She smiled and gave me a package wrapped in red tissue paper, then gave something to each of the boys.

I untied the thread. "Oh, Mum!" Inside was a length of shimmering yellow silk, lavishly embroidered with goldfish in shades of bronze and gray. I spread it on the bed and ran my hand over it.

"One of our Chinese church friends, Miss Wang, helped me get it," she explained.

"It's beautiful! Thank you so much."

"What's this?" Simeon asked, holding up his present. There were two sticks with a cord fastened to the ends, and a top made of two separate slotted bamboo cylinders connected by a piece of dowel.

Mum chuckled. "It's a top, a singing emperor. It'll take some practice, but I know you can do it." Simeon beamed. "It hums when you get it going fast enough."

"Look at these!" Benjamin exclaimed. "Me and Trevor can play." He held out a Chinese checkers game for us to see. "And you can play, too, if you want," he concluded generously, taking in the rest of us.

We gave Mum the presents we had brought. Benjamin's was a peculiar carving: a very wild panther, he explained; Simeon's was a springtime watercolor painting of the mountains around our school with the wild azaleas in bloom; and mine was a set of handkerchiefs I'd hemmed.

Simeon picked up the sticks to his singing emperor and tried to send the top up the cord and back. "I miss Dad," he said.

"Yes, I know," Mum answered. There was a commotion downstairs and someone called for her. "I'll have to see who that is."

Simeon went on practicing; Benjamin took off with his game to find Trevor; I folded my piece of silk.

"So much for Christmas," I said.

"They can't help it," Simeon said as he managed to get the top to move.

"I suppose."

That afternoon I asked Mum if Simeon and I could go out to look at the city. "No," she said regretfully.

"Why?" I asked.

"You wouldn't understand."

Old enough to help on the trip, I thought peevishly, but not old enough to hear explanations.

I went upstairs to our room. "Can you make the singing emperor hum?" I asked Simeon, seeing that he had set it aside.

"I got it to, a tiny bit," he said without looking up from what he was doing.

Benjamin and several little boys barged in and thrust a shiny tangle of wire at Simeon.

"Hey! Stop that, you dopes! You'll mess me up!" he exclaimed. In a cloth-lined basket beside him was a partly dismantled old black alarm clock. I went closer to see what he was doing, but he shielded his work with his arm. He was making a drawing in his careful way, but all I saw of it was two cog wheels. He closed his pad of paper, put it behind him, and looked in annoyance at the wire. "What do you want?" he asked.

"We made a telephone out of Trevor's mother's old zigzag-wire watchband and some more wire from a box in the laundry shed and these two cans," Benjamin told him. "Show him, Trev." Trevor held out a couple of

26

dull gray cans. "We made holes in the bottom with a nail."

"It doesn't work, does it?" Simeon asked, curious in spite of himself.

Trevor nodded enthusiastically, and his glasses slid up and down his nose.

"Kind of," Benjamin said. "But can you put it up in the hallway from my bed to Trevor's bed?"

"You're good at making things work," Trevor chirped. "Benjamin told me."

Benjamin smirked. "I did. I told him you always make things work."

Simeon eyed him and sighed. Most of that imp's compliments were transparently aimed at getting what he wanted. "Find me some thumbtacks," Simeon said, picking up his stuff, "and I will."

Late that night, I thought I had slipped into a nightmare. A light shone in my face, and an angry Chinese man's voice ordered me to get up. The command was repeated by several other voices. The light moved on to Simeon's and then to Benjamin's bed. I sat up, struggling to understand what was happening. "Hurry!" the first voice commanded us. I noticed that the faint green hands of our clock pointed to 11:30.

Simeon stumbled into the hall, but Benjamin didn't move. Shaking with fright, I reached under his arms and dragged him with me into the dimly lit hall, where the adults in their pajamas looked like strangely overgrown children. Dad was rubbing his chin as if he was quite upset, and Mum kept glancing at something near the ceiling. There was a strong smell of camphor oil from

27

one of the Goodnight Ladies, who kept mopping her nose and sneezing. She huddled back against the wall, trying to smother the noise.

The police officer with the thick glasses, who had checked our papers when we arrived, used his flashlight to point accusingly up at Benjamin's telephone wire. "Your father says it is yours. Show me where it goes. I know it is for spying." His three assistants glowered at Benjamin.

My mouth went dry. I looked at the men, horrified at their interpretation, then down at my groggy little brother. But Benjamin merely squinted at them, too sleepy to understand.

"Show them—" Dad started mildly.

"Not the father! The boy!" the men snapped.

"The telephone," Simeon prompted, and shook Benjamin's patched pajama sleeve.

Benjamin tilted back his head and, through his eyelashes, peered around at us all, still unable to wake up.

Dad shifted a little toward me. "Ruth, will you help him?" he asked in an undertone.

I took his small hand, hoping he wouldn't suddenly come to and make some unfortunate comment. "He will show you his toy in here," I said slowly and carefully for Benjamin's benefit.

The four men followed us into the bedroom. I lifted the pillow to show the can attached to the wire. One officer leaned over and curiously ran the tip of his finger around the rim. Then he straightened up and waited for Benjamin to demonstrate.

Simeon came in. "Show them how it works!" he said, and pushed it impatiently at our younger brother.

With a half-asleep frown on his face, Benjamin pressed the can to his ear, then pushed it against the leading policeman's shoulder. The man pressed it to his own long-lobed ear. Right away, Benjamin woke up entirely and laughed. Trevor snickered from the doorway. I wanted to clap my hand over my little brother's mouth, but I knew that would look suspicious. I squeezed his hand more tightly and stepped on his foot, but he laughed harder and started to point toward Trevor's room. "Let me show him"—he spluttered—"let me show him how . . ." He was too convulsed with laughter to finish.

The officer took an angry step. His black eyes glittered. "Western capitalists! Enemies of the People's Republic of China! American spies!" The scratchy voice grated on for several minutes. "Therefore, take it down and give it to me," he finished.

Simeon found a stool to stand on, and took the can, then pulled out the brass thumbtacks and dropped them in with a *plink, plink, plink*. He wound the wire along the hall to Trevor's bed, where he pulled out the other can, and held it all toward the man. The hall light went out. "Oh, dear. Not again. That's the third time, and it's supposed to be our good week," somebody murmured behind me. The city was divided into four sections: one week a month, there was more or less adequate electricity for one of the sections, and the rest of the time there might be light and there might not.

The policeman shone his flashlight around and snatched the cans from Simeon. "Never make mockery like this again," he snapped, and marched noisily down the stairs, followed by the other officers and by Mum and Dad.

Sniggers, tears, whispers, and shuffling feet sounded

in the sudden darkness as we made our way back to our room.

"Silly old duffers," Simeon mumbled through the blankets he had pulled over his head.

"Important me!" Benjamin chortled. "I'm a clever American spy!" His giggles popped through the darkness.

"Shut up," Simeon whispered harshly.

I lay shivering in the cold sheets. I pictured the dull, lead-colored cans with the odds and ends of wire strung from them, and the officers' angry faces. I knew they'd seen very little modern equipment, but even so, such profound suspicion over such a piece of childish junk didn't make much sense to me. These police and soldiers certainly are a strange bunch, I thought, or crazy, or something.

They'd been turning up the last few months at school, too, interrupting classes, delaying hockey games. We never knew what they were looking for, since they confiscated the oddest things: a piece of new chalk, a windup toy car, a pocket knife.

The teachers had tried to make sense of it for us, to help us understand why the Chinese thought we were so amusing during the Second World War but now treated us as enemies of some kind. During that war, China and the United States had been friendly allies, but after the war the United States turned its back on the new China and its leader Mao Tse-tung. Mao became allied to Stalin's Russia, and the United States refused to recognize either Mao or the People's Republic of China. The whole situation had grown worse this past June with the war in Korea, during which the two countries became open antagonists: China, North Korea, and Russia against the United States and South Korea.

What on earth do these police think my parents can spy out that could be used in Korea, I wondered. How long have Mum and Dad put up with this sort of thing? Why can't some of the other missionaries take care of things? I wanted to ask Mum and Dad, but I wasn't used to questioning adults about much of anything. At school, we talked to teachers in class. Occasionally they organized "private interviews" with us when we were supposed to discuss our concerns, but I always felt stiff and self-conscious and couldn't think what to say.

After a while, my parents came to bed. Mum said something to Dad, but I couldn't hear her words. "Tomorrow morning," he answered in a low voice. "I'll have to go right after breakfast."

五

FIVE

By our tenth day home, I knew something must be really wrong. That morning, Mum and Dad had assigned us regular jobs as if they expected us to be around for some time. Mine was to milk the cow, which was tied to a pomelo tree, kitty-corner to the well at the back of the house. Mum had come out to give me a quick lesson. "Here, try this," she'd said, demonstrating as she chanted. "Press at the top, squeeze down. Press at the top, squeeze down." After she left, I sat on the bamboo stool and repeated the rhythmic words.

Footsteps came up behind me and I glanced over my shoulder. Simeon again, I thought—he really is at loose ends. He'd been following me around for the past few days. I leaned back and stretched my cramped hands wide; there was only half an inch of milk in the bottom of the bucket.

"Is this your job now?" he asked. "I have to do the pump. With Benjamin, worse luck."

"I thought I could do this, but it's harder than it looks." I watched my right hand press evenly down the udder again. Steam curled off the milk. "You know, there's something funny about their giving us regular jobs for a short holiday."

"Yeah, it is funny." Simeon leaned against a wooden box of bran for the cow. "Did you know Dad went to the police station this morning? I wanted to go with him, but—"

"That's the third time in the last few days," I interrupted. "Don't you wish he'd tell us more?"

"Who?"

"Dad, you dodo, who else are we talking about?"

Simeon looked puzzled. "Tell us what?"

"About why he has to go to the police station all those times, and what he does in his study all day. And—oh, I don't know," I went on in frustration. "Just about what's happening."

"Why would you want to know all that?" Simeon asked.

"Sim!" I exploded. I stopped milking and looked up at him. "Aren't you even curious?"

He shrugged. "Dad's taking care of it." He paused a minute. "I don't think I want to know." He pulled a splinter of wood off the rough bran-box lid. "You could ask Dad if you want to know so badly."

"Ask him! I couldn't ask him." I turned back to my milking. "I wonder what Paul and Anne are doing at school," I said, changing to a safer subject. There was always a group of kids who, for one reason or another, stayed at school for the holidays. Usually we were among them, but this time it was my friend Anne and Simeon's friend Paul who were left behind.

"Mmm," he said. "I wish they could have come with us."

"Me, too." A sudden longing hit me as a picture of Anne with her laughing blue eyes and unruly red curls flashed across my mind. I remembered one day after a

33

particularly muddy game of field hockey, when we had been walking back to the dorm. We had passed Simeon sitting on a low wall. "Fancy seeing you and it's only Tuesday!" I had said. We laughed and looked awkwardly at each other, not sure what else to say, strangers now in the large boarding school. As we went on, good old Anne had commented sympathetically, "Funny, isn't it, the way he and Paul were always with us when the school was small. Now that it's big, we just see them at church on Sundays."

I knew Anne would have understood my disappointment in Simeon, which was sort of like putting on a favorite pair of comfortable old shoes and feeling wretched because they no longer fit the way they used to. We've been together the three weeks on the journey home and more than a week here, I thought dejectedly, but it still isn't the way it used to be.

"I never thought a holiday could get boring," Simeon broke in on my thoughts. "We hardly see Mum and Dad."

"I know. Sometimes it doesn't seem worth being home."

"Oh, I didn't mean that!" Simeon exclaimed. "Not at all. Anything is better than being at school." He was quiet a minute, then went on, "But all those wretched little kids, and Benjamin's the worst. They're so noisy, and on top of us all the time."

I smiled into the bucket. "Mmm. Benjamin is rather dreadful, but nice-dreadful. Nothing seems to bother him."

"I guess," he answered sadly. That tone, which always crept into his voice when I expressed fondness for Benjamin, made me feel hollow but also irked me. He's just stupidly jealous, I thought. I went on milking, and the *ting* of the spray hitting the side of the pail grew more regular. "Where'd this cow come from?" Simeon finally asked.

I laughed. "One of the missionaries had to bring it with him from his village. He's leaving the country, and because he didn't have a bill of sale, he couldn't sell it or give it away or butcher it. Some silly new government rule." I got up, stretched, and picked up the pail. "What do you want to do?"

"I *did* want Dad to help me fix that clock. You want to play checkers?"

"For the seventy-seventh time this week?" We left the bucket in the kitchen and went into the hall. Absently, Simeon straightened a rather hideous engraving of the coronation of Queen Victoria which hung near the door.

"Remember that cliff we walked to near school?" I asked. "Where those soldiers were squirting mouthfuls of water and making rainbows and—"

Benjamin whizzed by. We flattened ourselves against the wall, knocking the picture cockeyed again.

"Lion's Leap," Simeon reminded me.

"Yes. And wasn't Emerald Grotto with those three waterfalls beautiful?"

Trevor rushed past. We flattened ourselves against the wall.

"And Joe the Madman's Gazebo where we weren't allowed anymore," Simeon added. "I wonder why?"

"Oh, some military reason or something. And remember the Cave of the Immortals with that old priest," I went on. Simeon turned and nudged the corner of the frame with his thumb.

James, Ivan, and Danny zoomed by.

35

"We sure go to school near some spectacular pla—"

"Mmm," Simeon interrupted. "But I'm still glad we're here."

Mum came briskly up to us, a dozen forks raised ominously in her right fist. "Ruth, Simeon, round those boys up and get them outside." But she couldn't look really cross: her face had too many smile creases for that. Feet pounded overhead and stopped with a thump. A scrap of plaster landed on Mum's shoulder. "I feel like the old woman who lived in a shoe." There were three more thumps overhead.

"With a shoeful of kids screeching and banging about," I added. "Where are the other parents?"

Mum's brown eyes flashed. "Improving their spirits. Praying and reading their Bibles, when they should be curbing their young." As she gestured toward the living room, I noticed she was wearing a ring I hadn't remembered.

"We'll get them, Mum," I told her, sensing her predicament. We went upstairs; I took the right hall and Simeon the left. Along the right-hand hall, between two bedrooms, a narrow staircase led to the attic. Several little boys crouched there in the shadows. I reached for Ivan and Danny. "Come on, you jokers. You're to go outside now."

"But Benjamin said we're playing all over the house!" Trevor argued.

"Sounds like him," I said, "but he's got another thing coming." I yanked them along to the end of the other upstairs hall. The clatter of all their shoes on the bare floorboards sounded like a herd of goats being driven over a plank bridge. Doors opened and the stern faces of several single missionaries looked disapprovingly out. At the end of the hallway, we bumped into Simeon, who had snagged Benjamin.

"She says we can't play all over the house," Trevor announced in a disgruntled voice.

"Then what can we do?" Benjamin challenged me.

"You can play ball." I pushed them through the door onto the back veranda. "Go on," I ordered Benjamin. "Get the ball."

"Don't know where it is," Benjamin retorted and tossed me a saucy grin.

"Well, find it, you twit."

Before long, a game of dodgeball jolted into action.

Somewhere nearby, a baby cried. I went toward the sound. "Aren't you coming?" Simeon asked. "To play checkers?"

"I'll be along in a jiff," I told him. In the kitchen, in a box on the table, was a beautiful baby, just a few weeks old. "Oh, what a lovely baby! Is he yours?" I asked the cook's wife.

She smiled with shy pride. "He is our son!"

"May I look after him sometime?"

She looked uneasy. "Ask your family," she advised me uncomfortably.

I looked longingly at the baby, not sure what my mother's answer would be, then left to find Simeon. Somebody in the yard screamed and a second later glass tinkled. "You looney!" one of the boys yelled.

Simeon and I went to the dining room, where Mum stood with a large glass water jug in her hand, sighing over the broken window. Through the jagged hole we could see the yard filling with scolding parents, while the silent little boys stared at the damage.

"Well, Mum," I suggested, "there's your clue to getting those parents moving."

She gave me a squashed smile. "It's naughty of me to laugh."

"Mum," I asked, "is that a new ring? I don't remember it." I touched the narrow gold band set with sparkly red garnets.

She smiled as if she enjoyed the recollection. "Every now and then your father gets very romantic."

"Dad gave it to you! What for?"

"For love," Mum said, a little embarrassed, then added quickly, "We had a holiday in the mountains just after Benjamin went to school, before starting here in Chengtu. He gave it to me then."

"Did you give him something?"

She laughed. "I tried to knit him a sweater, but I made it big enough for us both to fit in!"

The front door creaked slowly open and slowly closed; heavy footsteps followed and stopped. Mum set down the water jug. "That must be Gideon," she said, and hurried to see if it was Dad. Simeon and I followed.

He stood near the door, rubbing his thumb along his lower lip and looking down at a bunch of papers in his hand. "I don't know," he said, without noticing that Simeon and I were behind Mum. "The police won't say yes and they won't say no. This one asked that one, and that one went through the papers. Then they both went out to find someone else . . ."

Mum gave a short, sympathetic laugh. "Maybe the children will have to stay."

"I'm beginning to think so, especially because the gatekeeper—"

Simeon moved next to Dad. "You mean it?" he asked eagerly. "We won't have to go back for quite a while?"

Dad looked up blankly, as if he'd just realized what Simeon had heard. "Probably not," he answered slowly. "Here's what the gatekeeper handed me." In a rare gesture of explanation, Dad held out a smeary grayish telegram from the school: *Keep children until notified.* "That must mean the school is having new troubles with more government restrictions. So even if we could sort things out with the police here, you probably can't go back."

Simeon beamed.

I stared at the telegram and at the useless papers in Dad's hands. Since our school had such a chaotic history, it had never occurred to me that it might close entirely. Anne will go to her people in New Zealand, I thought bleakly. I'll never see her again. I'll have no friend, nobody to talk to.

"Well, lunch is ready. Come along," Mum said briskly. "Go ring the bell for the first shift, Ruth."

SIX

By midafternoon I wanted something to take my mind off the craziness of everything, which looked as if it was getting worse instead of better. I found my mother outside the linen cupboard and asked her, "May I go down to the cook's house to see their baby?" I knew it wasn't the usual thing to do; at school we were forbidden to visit the servants at all.

Mum sighed and didn't answer right away. "They bring him up here sometimes," she said tentatively.

"I know, but he's not here now. May I?"

She thought a little longer. "Well, I suppose it's all right this time."

"Thank you," I said, and hurried down the path through the bamboo grove. On the other side was a small, gray-tiled house with whitewashed walls where the cook and his wife lived. I knocked and waited.

A very pretty girl with long black braids tied with red yarn, eighteen or nineteen years old, opened the door. In her left arm she carried the baby.

"Oh!" I said, taken by surprise. "I'm Ruth. From there." I pointed up the path. "I thought Wu Da-sao was here. I came to see the baby."

The girl looked curiously at me. "Come in. Come in,"

she said with an eager friendliness that startled me. "Wu Da-sao isn't here, but I am Chuin-mei, a relative. Would you like to hold him?"

I stepped inside, sat on the stool Chuin-mei pushed forward, and took the well-bundled baby. "Have you come to help?" I asked.

"I visit now and then. Your sweater is very pretty."

I was puzzled by the unnecessary compliment. The sweater was thick and gray, with blue stripes every three inches, and not particularly attractive. "I guess so," I said awkwardly.

"The baby is a fine one," Chuin-mei commented.

"Yes. And he's a boy: the cook and his wife are very pleased."

"That's old China when girls were worthless." She grimaced as if remembering something hateful. "Our new government treats girls the same as boys," Chuin-mei informed me.

I gawked. "You like the way the Communists do things?" I asked thoughtlessly.

She tossed one braid back over her shoulder and leaned toward me. "The Government of the People is the only one that truly serves all the people," she began earnestly. "It is the rule of the masses. We are all working together to improve ourselves. We will solve our problems. We will build our country through industriousness and thrift." Her voice settled into a singsong political-rally cadence. "Through the united efforts of all our people working with our own hands, China will become strong. China will become prosperous."

For a minute I was taken aback by this volley of information, although it was not unlike some of the religious homilies I had heard one small question trigger. "Is this all you think about?" I asked.

"It is all everyone thinks about!" she told me, wide-eyed with amazement. "What do *you* think of government?"

I frowned, knowing I couldn't match her explanation. "I don't know," I said. "It's all very confusing." I covered my embarrassment by rocking the baby back and forth, watching his perfect little face, but uncomfortably aware of Chuin-mei's eyes on me. "To me," I started hesitantly, "governments are like books of rules which somebody tore apart a long time ago. Some pages are lost and the rest are mixed up, so nobody can use them properly." I swallowed, trying to think of how to continue.

Chuin-mei waited quietly.

"Of course, lots of people have tried, so you read what one person says and that seems right. Then you read the opposite, and that seems just as right." I sighed, recalling some of the confusing discussions in school about monarchies, oligarchies, democracies, and whatever the rest of them were. I had never really thought much about government; it was just one of those things that was there.

I glanced up, but Chuin-mei looked puzzled, so I toiled on, wondering if I was making any sense to her. "Then there's an uprising or a civil war or a revolution or something, and what is written seems more muddled than ever. They say, 'Do this and everything will be fine,' and it isn't."

I put my finger in the baby's tiny fist. "I guess God and the people who really study that sort of thing can see some kind of order, but I sure can't," I ended help-lessly.

"But Chairman Mao is making a new book for China," Chuin-mei said. She watched me closely, as if waiting for a comment, but I knew I was already out of my depth. Then she went on, "What do you think of America fighting in Korea?"

"All war is ghastly," I answered, frightened by the question. "I should go now," I said abruptly, and stood up, holding out the bundle of baby and blankets.

He whimpered and she took him and put the knuckle of her little finger in his mouth. "I hope I see you next time I come?"

"Perhaps," I answered, pleased by her interest, but also wary.

To have a friend! I thought longingly, as I kicked a pebble along the path toward the main house. Chuin-mei certainly wasn't like Anne, but then nobody could be. I hadn't had a Chinese friend since I was little. I stopped at the edge of the bamboo grove and toyed with the idea. Chuin-mei's eager, friendly face made me smile to myself as I imagined us playing with the baby, talking about . . . I wasn't sure what—I hoped not the sober topics we'd just tried.

Later that afternoon, I was idly poking through a basket of socks Mum had asked me to mend. Mixed in with them were cards of assorted mending threads, spools of black and white threads, and an old envelope of embroidery floss of various colors. I put my hand down one tan sock, not really paying attention to the hole that spread over the back of my hand. I wondered what work

Chuin-mei did; or if she was taking some sort of political studies; and if she had brothers and sisters; and if she'd been to school and if—there were so many things I wanted to know.

Just then Mum hurried up to me. "Where's the supper milk?" she asked.

For a minute I looked blankly at her. "I forgot," I said guiltily. "I'm sorry. I'll go do it now." I pulled off the sock, shoved it back in the basket, and followed her into the kitchen for the bucket.

"You're your mother's daughter," she said with a short laugh.

"What do you mean?" I asked.

"Forgetting, forgetting," she said.

七

SEVEN

Chuin-mei was a magnet. By the end of January, I had only been to visit her a few times. But even so, when I wasn't with Chuin-mei, I often thought about her, wondering if maybe we could be friends. She was so different from the missionary kids I knew and I was intrigued.

"What's the matter with you?" Simeon asked one morning, when I was milking the cow.

I took my forehead away from the cow's flank and looked up, puzzled. "What do you mean?"

"I've said your name three times and you haven't answered. What's happened to you lately? You're off in a fog somewhere."

"Isn't it," I started. "Wouldn't it . . . I mean, don't you wish we could have new friends here?"

"New friends?" he questioned.

"You know, kids our age?"

He frowned at me. "You *are* acting funny," he said unhappily. "You know there aren't any kids our age here."

I hadn't told my parents about my visits to the cook's house, or about my growing fondness for Chuin-mei. I knew it was all right for little Chinese kids and little Western kids to play together, but I wasn't little anymore.

And Mum had been so reluctant when I'd first asked to see the baby, I was afraid they wouldn't approve.

Now, I suddenly realized, I didn't want to tell Simeon either: he might not understand and he might tell.

There was shouting at the front gate. "Come on," I said impatiently. "Let's go see who that is—maybe it's someone interesting for a change." I got up and grabbed the milk pail. Simeon followed me to the front veranda, where we stood behind a pillar to watch.

A gray-haired woman came through the gate, and then a man. "Here, David," she said, and handed something to him. His face made me think of the Biblical David, who was "ruddy and withal of a beautiful countenance, and goodly to look to." The new missionary was young and slender, and he had very blue eyes and curly dark hair. He was dressed, not in the usual gray or brown suit, but in an ankle-length black quilted Chinese gown. He walked purposefully toward the house, carrying a heavy old suitcase. I wondered frivolously if this handsome man ever got himself into passionate and interesting difficulties, the way the historic David had.

Just as he neared the veranda, an old soccer ball flew toward him, with Benjamin swooping after it, nearly toppling the man.

"Just a minute, little boy," he said. I was disappointed—his voice didn't fit the rest of him. Instead of being dramatically deep and full as I had imagined, it was a tenor voice: clear, precise, and definite. His foot, in a Chinese cloth shoe, stepped firmly on the ball.

Benjamin hunkered beside it, then raised his head inch by inch, working his way up the man's long gown, until he reached the stern new face. "It's our ball!" he said indignantly.

"Now think," the man said. "What do you say when you've nearly knocked a person over?"

Benjamin was silent.

"He doesn't know Benjamin," I snickered to Simeon, and bumped him with the milk pail.

"Benjamin's just rude," Simeon groused.

Our little brother stared up at the man. "Excuse me, please, sir," he answered, startled that someone he didn't know would reprimand him like this.

"That's better." The man took his foot off the ball and looked intently beyond Benjamin to the edge of the house where four more little boys peered at him. "Enough for a school, I see."

Benjamin took a deep breath. "School!" he protested. "We're on holiday!"

I whispered to Simeon, "Good. That'll keep those little demons busy."

"Maybe we can think of something to do if they're out of the way," he answered.

"David, you are incorrigible," the woman said in an amused, gravelly voice. Simeon and I stared in surprise at a woman reprimanding a man. She was a big work-horse of a woman with a wilderness of gray hair contained by bone hairpins. Her eyes were brown, with fan creases at their corners. In her thick hands she carried a large old purse covered entirely in black-bead embroidery. She stooped and put one hand on Benjamin's shoulder. A loose string of the tiny black beads caught in his hair. He shifted back a little. "Mark my words, young man, if my brother says you're having school, you'll have school. Even though we hope to be here only a week or so." She smiled, reached out, and disentangled the beads from his hair.

Benjamin grinned back and tore off with the ball. "But not me!" he called over his shoulder.

Her brother! I thought. There were quantities of single women missionaries, but single men were a rarity.

Suddenly the clasp on the man's battered leather suitcase gave way and everything spilled out. There were several more gowns, which he had used to wrap half a dozen or more thick books, and a collection of Chinese calligraphy brushes. He stooped and gathered everything up, carefully rewrapping each book before putting it back, then held the case together with both hands.

When he reached the veranda, he caught sight of Simeon and me. "Two more!" he commented in a pleased voice.

I frowned, unsure what he meant.

"For school," he explained, as if he could read my mind.

"Aren't we rather old to be in with that lot?" I asked.

"A spread of ages is valuable. The older ones can help the younger ones." I blinked—he sounded as if he'd appropriated us all, and I wasn't even sure what to call him yet. The two of them went on into the house.

"It's just a week," Simeon said as we walked to the kitchen with the milk pail.

"That's what they hope, like quite a few people who've been here a month or more." I didn't know whether to be annoyed, pleased, or amused.

* * *

A couple of days later Mr. Hilary began his school. He led us all up the narrow, seldom-used stairs to the only spare room in the house. It was a small attic room with cracked plaster walls and a sloping roof. Two crows peered down through a skylight. Somebody had tried to dust and sweep it all.

We crowded around a wooden trestle table which almost filled the room. I slumped awkwardly on the bench, feeling like a hulk next to all the small children.

Mr. Hilary waited until we were settled, then bowed his head to avoid hitting the skylight, and sat down, very erect, at the end of the table. I watched him curiously. He looked around at each of us as if he was pleased with the prospect of teaching, then passed out very thin sheets of airmail paper on which something was typed. Mine, which was the last carbon copy, was very faint.

Benjamin squinted at his. "This looks like a poem. What's it for?"

"It *is* a poem, the work of the great Wordsworth: 'I wandered lonely as a cloud.' "

Benjamin's rosy face crinkled into laughter. "What's a poem for?"

"You're memorizing it tonight."

Briefly, he looked alarmed, then stared impishly at Mr. Hilary. "I don't memorize poems."

"Nor me," Trevor added. "And anyhow I'm leaving soon."

"Benjamin." Mr. Hilary made his name echo with reproaches.

I bit my cheeks to keep from laughing and glanced

across at Simeon, but he was staring moodily at the brown pencil stub in his hands.

"This is supposed to be our holiday," Benjamin grumped. "Nobody memorizes poems during holidays." He gave the bench leg a kick.

"Your holiday was slated to end in the middle of January, and it's already February. Until the police grant my sister and me permission to go on, I will instruct this band of scholars."

"Not all poems!" Benjamin groaned.

"No." Mr. Hilary patted the fat brown text in front of him. "There's enough in here to last us a while, supplemented by material from my memory." As he raised his arm, the sleeve of his gown caught the cover of the book and twitched it open. The type was dismayingly fine.

Benjamin leaned forward and frowned, trying to read the title at the top of the page. He lifted the cover and read the spine: *"The Poor Man's* . . . What's that word, Trev?"

Trevor tilted his glasses. *"Library."*

Benjamin dropped the cover in disgust. "Botheration!" he muttered. Then he looked up and grinned. "Oh, well, you said you'll be here just a week."

Mr. Hilary gave him an amused glance. "First we'll read this poem together," he said.

At the end of our lessons, I went to the dining room. "What do you think of your peculiar schoolmaster?" Mum asked me as she finished pouring water into the glasses in preparation for lunch.

I chuckled. "He'll certainly be interesting." I fidgeted

with my fingers. "How long are we going to be doing this? I mean, staying here like this?"

Mum gave me a troubled look and shook her head. "I don't know, Ruth," she said in a voice that told me I shouldn't ask any more questions.

八

EIGHT

Later that day, I walked anxiously down the path toward the cook's house and stopped just inside the bamboo grove. Although I sort of enjoyed the secrecy surrounding my visits with Chuin-mei, it also made me nervous and uncomfortable. It wasn't just the uncertainty of what my parents would think; it was also that Wu Da-sao accepted me in a rather uneasy way, and Chuin-mei frequently brought up things I wanted to avoid.

Rain began to fall. One drop trickled coldly down my neck. Off to the right Trevor's mother was hastily taking down socks from the line. If only Simeon weren't so out of sorts and the others weren't so tiresomely young, I thought. If only there was someone else my age. I guess I'll try once more, I decided, and walked on.

When I knocked, Wu Da-sao called for me to come in. "Is Chuin-mei here?" I asked.

The cook's wife stopped pushing the needle through the cloth shoe sole she was making, nodded grudgingly, and motioned toward the bedroom. Chuin-mei came out, carrying the baby. She wore the usual tan jacket and pants. She looked tired and her chin was chapped.

I smiled eagerly at her. "Have you been working out of doors?"

52

Her face brightened. "Carrying stones."

"Carrying stones!"

She came a step nearer, her face shining. "For the river-deepening project. We all are working with our hands for the improvement of our country," she said with pride. "Hundreds of women with shoulder poles and baskets carry stones from the river to a road the soldiers are building."

"To where?"

"I don't know," she answered abruptly.

"It seems funny to do all that work and not know where the road will go."

Chuin-mei pursed her lips. I knew I'd said the wrong thing again. She lifted the baby to her shoulder, turned to a shelf behind the table, and picked up some fabric stretched over a bamboo hoop. She brought it to where I was awkwardly standing near the door. "Would you like to learn to embroider?" she asked as she held it out to me.

I ran my finger around the border of a red chrysan-themum, exquisitely stitched. "It's beautiful, but I could never do anything like that!"

"It is bad," Chuin-mei said with Oriental modesty. "But I can teach you."

I shrugged. "Might as well try," I said uncertainly, and went back to the house. Maybe this will make visits more comfortable, I thought—keep us off politics. And Mum will probably be less annoyed if I'm learning some-thing. I found one of my white blouses and the envelope of embroidery thread from the sewing basket, and re-turned with them.

Chuin-mei, who was sitting on the bench by the table,

exchanged the baby for the blouse. She motioned for me to sit on a stool, and then began to draw an outline of fruit and leaves on the fabric.

"What fruit is it?" I asked when she had finished. "I don't recognize those leaves."

"A persimmon. It is the symbol of friendship."

I smiled, very pleased. "I like that."

"If I teach you this, will you teach me English?" Until now, our conversations had been in Chinese.

"What kind?" I asked warily. I couldn't think why she'd want to learn English, since most Westerners were being sent out of the country.

"All kinds," she answered. "What is this?" She put the tip of her finger on the baby's tiny nose.

"Nose," I said.

"No-se." Chuin-mei repeated the awkward word, then ruffled the baby's silky black hair.

"Hair."

"Hai-r."

"Ear."

"Ea-r."

"Mouth." The baby opened his lips and chewed Chuin-mei's finger. We glanced at each other and giggled tentatively, then harder, helplessly. The tension and vague suspicion evaporated.

Wu Da-sao, who had been working on her shoe and ignoring us entirely, frowned. "You are women! You act like silly children," she scolded. The baby's face grew red and he started to howl. His mother took him and carried him into the bedroom. The heavy blue curtain which served as a door dropped behind her.

Immediately, as if she'd made a sudden decision, Chuin-mei's face grew serious. She anxiously clutched one of her braids, leaned closer, and whispered, "Sometimes when you see me you won't understand what I do, but remember, I am always your friend." She held out both hands.

Impulsively, I took her hands, almost as if making a vow. "And I am your friend. But what—" Wu Da-sao returned and picked up her work.

Shortly afterwards, I got up to go. "Will I see you in church on Sunday?" I asked Wu Da-sao, laughing because last week, when the congregation started singing a particularly boisterous hymn, the baby had cried so loudly she got up and left with him. Wu Da-sao gave me a funny look and muttered something I didn't hear. I shrugged and went back to the main house.

That night, I lay in bed feeling a quiet excitement over the promise Chuin-mei and I had made. I dropped off to sleep but kept waking, and finally got up for a drink of water. I was puzzled to see Mum and Dad's bed still empty.

At the oil lamp on the landing, I met one of the Good-night Ladies in her bathrobe, coming from the other hall. "You can't sleep, either?" she asked. I shook my head. "I hear voices," she continued, turning toward the sound. "That's nice. I'll go and join them." She went on toward Dad's study.

Poor Mum and Dad, I thought. Even in the middle of the night they can't be alone.

It wasn't until Sunday that I remembered Mum and Dad's discussion, which took place so strangely late; and Wu Da-sao's odd behaviour when I'd mentioned church.

55

Instead of going to the Chinese church next door, the missionaries and their families were gathering in the living room. "What's happening?" I asked Mum. "Why are we meeting here?"

"We're an embarrassment. To the Chinese Christians," she said abruptly.

"Embarrassment?"

She hesitated. Sometimes I had the feeling she would have explained more if she hadn't been so utterly loyal to Dad. "Spies, the new government calls us, and plenty else." Mum made a frustrated gesture and sat down. "We don't want to make it look as if the Chinese church folk are harboring dangerous political—"

Her last word was swallowed by a roar which sounded like an airplane. Although that seemed unlikely, it was enough to trigger my memories of planes and bombing. I sat tensely on my chair.

During the second prayer, which I found hard to follow, Benjamin started dropping first his Bible, then his hymnbook. He picked them up and dropped them again. After the third or fourth time, Simeon grabbed them away from him. Another roar overhead—I was now certain it was a plane—drowned out his whispered retort. Alexandra's father began his sermon. "God wants us to—" Trevor fell off the sofa and banged his head. His howl was stifled by another roar. Planes were passing at five-minute intervals, near enough to make the house shake.

I glanced at Simeon and knew that he remembered the bombing, too, from when we were at school in Loshan. He was biting his nails in an agitated way I thought he had outgrown. With his other hand, he clutched the Bibles and hymnbooks on his lap.

Alexandra's father broke off in the middle of his sermon. "There's not much point in going on," he said. The little children tore outside, and the adults followed more sedately. I avoided looking at Simeon, not wanting to expose my fear, and followed the others outside.

Everyone stood about with heads tilted to the heavy, leaden sky. Three planes, like immense molting crows, swept low over the city, dropping black leaflets.

Uneasily, Simeon and I watched the younger children running about with their hands held high, trying to catch the fluttering leaflets, then diving at the ground to grab as many as possible.

"I got two!"

"I got six!"

"I got one!"

"What's it say?" Benjamin gave a pile to Dad. We could speak Chinese but could read only a few characters.

Grimly, Dad read the white print on a black leaflet. "Hate America! Help Korea! Down with the capitalist spies! Chase out the American robbers!"

From next door came the voices of the Chinese Christians singing the Twenty-third Psalm. I felt sad and comforted and scared all at once.

"What about this one?"

He read it. "The same."

"And this?"

He glanced over it. "The same."

"All of them?"

Dad shuffled through them, started to pass them back,

but then changed his mind. "All of them." He frowned at them as if reading an ominous letter. "It's even more evident our work here is over," he said to himself, then finished with something about ". . . deliberate choice of church time." Simeon sidled over as if to show he cared, but Dad was too preoccupied to notice him.

Benjamin squinted up at Dad. "Who are the American robbers?" he asked.

"That's what they call us."

"Us!" Benjamin was about to laugh, but Dad's expression stopped him.

"What'll you do?" I asked.

"God alone knows," Dad moaned. He threw down the leaflets with a kind of despair and walked quickly back into the house. A roar drowned the banging of the door.

Slowly Benjamin gathered up the leaflets. From next door, old carpenter Liu's loud voice, always lagging a little behind the rest, finished the hymn.

At bedtime Dad came upstairs with Mum to say good night. When they sat down on their bed, I knew something serious must have happened. Dad pursed his lips, frowned for a while, and finally started talking. "Most of the rest of the mission has left China. We've decided the time has come for us to leave, too."

"Leave!" Benjamin exclaimed. "Tomorrow? Where are we going?"

"Hong Kong. But—" Again Dad frowned and seemed unable to find the words he wanted. He cupped his hands over his knees and stared down. What is the matter with him, I thought impatiently; he never used to be like this. "We don't know how long it will take," he explained. "It could be a few weeks. It could be a year or more. We just don't know. But let's commit this country and ourselves to God." Mum moved closer to Dad and he began to pray.

I didn't close my eyes as the others did. Instead, I stared at my parents, sitting side by side in the poor light with their heads bowed. They looked overwhelmed, defeated, crushed. Or did they? Why couldn't they explain more? Why couldn't we just leave and make our way along until we got to Hong Kong, the way we had when we children came from school? Or had the rules changed to make that impossible? I tried to concentrate on Dad's prayers, but I couldn't. I felt as if I was working one of those mazes where the player keeps dodging down blind alleys.

My parents left the room. Ignoring Benjamin's and Simeon's excited chatter, I lay in the dark, imagining Chuin-mei—her friendship seemed the only worthwhile thing in my life.

九

NINE

Week after week went by, with missionaries arriving from the outstations and other groups leaving, but for some inscrutable reason, none of the families with children from school were given permission to go. Once, Dad really lit into Benjamin, who'd been pesty with his questions about our leaving. All Mum ever answered was a harassed "I don't know."

I waited for a chance to ask Chuin-mei what she meant by her strange comment about something I wouldn't understand, but Wu Da-sao was always in the room. I didn't tell Chuin-mei our plans to go to Hong Kong, partly because they hardly seemed like plans and partly because my feelings about leaving were mixed. Part of me wanted to go, but part of me was afraid to go because I had spent most of my life in China and wasn't looking forward to living somewhere strange. I could not imagine Chuin-mei understanding such indecisiveness.

Nobody took us anywhere, and we weren't allowed out on our own. If it hadn't been for Mr. Hilary's school, I don't know what we'd have done with ourselves.

One morning toward the end of March, Mr. Hilary assigned us work to do while he was busy discussing something with Dad. As soon as his footsteps faded, the attic classroom burst into chatter.

"Hush up," I said after a while. "You're supposed to be working, and I can't label this picture if you're all babbling." I found it hard to concentrate on the names of the parts of the plant I was copying onto an enlarged diagram. "Features of the umbelliferae, carrot family. A, compound umbel of Pseudotaenidia montana; B, flower of Chaerophyllum procumbens." Benjamin slid off the end of the bench and peered over my right arm. "Move off, you old silly, you're bumping me. Why are you so interested anyway?" I asked.

He snickered, leaned comfortably toward my ear, and spoke in a moist whisper. Then he straightened and gave Trevor an exaggerated wink.

I wiped my ear, chuckled, and turned to Simeon. "Do you know their plan?"

"Yes, and I said maybe I'd help, but you're in charge while he's downstairs, and it's you he'll get after," he said peevishly.

"Maybe you're right, and anyway it's not very safe." I knew I should flatly forbid it, but the prank would break the monotony.

"Mr. H. is just an old duffer," Benjamin commented airily.

"I don't think so," I said. "And I don't know whether he can take a joke or not." Until now Mr. Hilary had seemed unflappable, but this prank was carrying things a little far.

"Come on," Benjamin urged. "You don't have to do anything. Just pretend you didn't see us."

I laughed. "That's a pretty big pretend." But I moved

Mr. Hilary's book out of the way. It was a navy-blue volume with faded gold lettering: *The Complete Works of William Wordsworth*. A sudden curiosity made me turn to the flyleaf. There was a dedication in a beautiful italic script such as we had learned in art class at school:

A man, Sir, should keep his friendship in constant repair.
S. Johnson, 1755

For David from Catherine. May 1941
I love you still.

How do you repair a friendship, I wondered vaguely, and what had happened between Mr. Hilary and his friend to provoke such a comment, and where was she now? The quote didn't sound romantic, but the postscript certainly did. I closed the book and put it down beside my diagram.

Benjamin helped Trevor lift a bench, which wobbled a bit when Simeon stood on it to open the skylight. I climbed up beside him. "See, it's safe," he said to me.

I glanced at him. He'd just told me I should stop them, and now here he was, eager to help the boys. I shrugged and looked down at the gray tiles. The roof sloped at a shallow angle, and about halfway down it was a wide bracket which fastened with rods to the ridge.

"It's a funny contraption," Simeon said. "I don't know what it's for, but it's perfect for this."

"I guess," I said doubtfully, and got out of their way.

A blast of chilly air wafted my diagram to the floor. "Come on. Hop up. Hurry!" Simeon hissed impatiently, lifting the little boys up to the roof one by one. "Don't move now. I'm coming." Just before he closed the skylight, he whispered tauntingly, "It's all yours, Ruth."

The window plopped shut and bits of black dirt scattered onto the table. Tiles grated, then everything was still. I put the bench back in place and picked up the diagram. Soft footsteps started up the attic stairs.

Aileen looked sullen. "Why didn't they let *us* up?"

"You wouldn't have dared," I whispered to her. "Shhh."

Slowly the door opened. Mr. Hilary came in and looked deliberately around the room. Several of the little girls snickered uneasily. "Ruth, I thought you were in charge," he said.

"Yes, sir," I answered, and continued copying, with my head low, to cover the foolishness I felt.

"Well?"

"It's a joke, sir." A tile on the roof grated, and I glanced quickly at him. He stood very still, listening.

"We do have to humor them a bit, I suppose." He gave a low chuckle.

We! I thought, and dropped my pencil in surprise. He was amused, and he had included me as an adult!

Several bits of dirt dropped to the table. Mr. Hilary reached up, tapped the skylight, and pushed it open cautiously. "Simeon, lift them over. I'll catch them."

But Simeon must not have heard, because there was a chorus of giggles as a flight of white paper planes drifted into the attic classroom. Then Benjamin's head hung down through the skylight, and almost knocked Mr. Hilary's. "How come you want to teach us?" Benjamin asked.

Mr. Hilary stepped back and answered the upside-down head. "I need work to do; you need to learn. So it's the perfect solution to a vexing situation. Come down now."

But that rapscallion wasn't through. "You mean it's not real, then? We don't have to do it anymore?" he asked eagerly.

"You have to do it. You know I've discussed it with all your parents."

"Botheration!" Benjamin grumbled, his face beet-red. He raised his head, put an arm across a corner of the skylight, and rested his cheek on it.

Mr. Hilary waited patiently with his face turned up.

"You could take us on walks instead," Benjamin suggested. "Explore the city, you know. We haven't been out for ages."

"Absolutely ages!" came an echo from the roof.

"It's not allowed," Mr. Hilary said. "We're under house arrest."

So that's what's happening, I thought. That's why every time we've wanted to go somewhere there's been some reason we couldn't. I looked at Mr. Hilary with new interest; he certainly was different from most adults.

"Come down now." He put up his hand to reach Benjamin.

When everyone else was back inside, Simeon knelt at the edge of the skylight and looked down with a worried frown. "I didn't hear you properly. Did you say"—he paused— "arrest?"

"House arrest," Mr. Hilary explained matter-of-factly. "All it means is that we have to get police permission whenever we want to go anywhere beyond the compound gates."

"But that's serious, sort of, isn't it?" Simeon persisted.

"We don't know what it means except that we're being watched."

After Simeon came down, Mr. Hilary surprised us by standing on the bench and putting his head through the skylight, looking out at the city. "I wonder if he ever played a prank like that when he was a kid," I whispered across the table to Simeon. But Simeon didn't answer.

Mr. Hilary's long, black quilted gown gave an occasional flap. The little girls sat hugging themselves against the chilly breeze. "I'm cold," Aileen whined.

"What's he doing?" Alexandra whispered.

Mr. Hilary fastened the skylight, stepped off the bench, and sat in his seat. "The parts of the seed," he said in Simeon's direction, "what are they? Now think."

"Huh?" Simeon answered distractedly. "Oh. You mean we're in class again now?" Mr. Hilary nodded. "Um. The coat."

"What is the technical name?"

"Um. The testa. Then there's the scar and that's called the, um, hilum."

"And it's like our tummy buttons," Benjamin burst out, "because it's where it broke off the bean pod."

"Yes, I suppose it is something like that," Mr. Hilary agreed.

Suddenly Benjamin grinned as we heard Mr. Bowser's labored clomping on the steps.

Sylvia's father was an American missionary, an ex-G.I., who was tackling our physical education. He had decided to teach us to march, as most Chinese school-children did. Simeon hadn't started to grow yet, so he didn't look as out of place as I did. I felt like a galumphing elephant, exercising with all those little ones, yet my submission to rules was so automatic I didn't think to ask to be excused.

We tumbled downstairs behind Mr. Bowser's broad back and onto the lawn. The others all threw their sweaters on the ground, but I was too embarrassed by my changing shape to take mine off when we trotted around the lawn.

"Line up! Two and two! On the double," Mr. Bowser commanded. He gestured out toward the middle of the lawn. Sylvia meandered about, looking for a partner, until she bumped into Aileen.

"First some simple marching. Straight ahead. All in step." We straggled forward. "Left now. Left! Left!" he shouted and signaled stormily to the left as Benjamin and Trevor headed off to the right. He ran up and herded us all to the left. "Jiminy crickets!" he exclaimed, and mopped his face with his handkerchief.

We had almost collided with a very disciplined double column of ten people arriving through the gate. The first two carried an impressive white banner with red characters. It was about the size of half a bedsheet, mounted on two bamboo poles. They held it high over their heads.

The brigade leader, a stocky woman with smallpox scars on her face, pushed importantly ahead of the carriers. "We are the Sanitation Brigade of the People's Republic of China." She glared at the front door and made her angry speech, one eye twitching as she spoke. "Flies cause sickness which kills brave Chinese who should go to fight the wicked Americans in Korea, who are spraying germs to kill innocent people."

She went on to outline the life cycle of the fly. Then she unrolled a poster and pointed to the enormous Chinese baby on it, with its mouth open wide enough to swallow the malicious oversized fly settled beside it. "We are in-

66

oculating against cholera. Roll up your sleeves." She snapped out the marching count and the brigade continued onto the veranda, where they set up a plank table and spread out kidney basins, hypodermics, cotton swabs, and bottles of vaccine.

Behind the table, a girl with a red cloth twisted around her wrist crouched over a temperamental alcohol burner to boil the needles. The girl was Chuin-mei! I imagined she must be proud to be part of the effort to make the country healthier, even if it took this form, which seemed rather strange to me.

Some of the littlest children began to cry. "Do we really have to have more injections?" Aileen whimpered. "We had them just before we left school." She shivered, partly from cold and partly from fear.

"Why do they do it like this?" James stuttered.

"Do you want me to go first?" I asked Mr. Bowser.

"No. No. I'll go," he said with firm cheerfulness. "They'll see it's not so bad." He rolled up his sleeve and bounded onto the veranda.

A little to one side of the table stood a pinch-mouthed health worker with no obvious duties. His eyes, which seemed to record every detail, slid over Mr. Bowser and down to Chuin-mei crouched over the alcohol burner.

She stood up with a needle clamped in bamboo tongs. I smiled. Chuin-mei looked at me but her face remained as expressionless as a propaganda poster. I dropped my smile and glanced apprehensively at the watching man. To my relief, he was frowning at the fellow working on Mr. Bowser.

He was a short man with a thickened red nose and cheeks, whose deliberate movements made me think he was listening to commands from inside his head. He swabbed Mr. Bowser's arm with an alarming thoroughness. The leading woman stepped smartly forward and tried to give Mr. Bowser the injection, but his skin was tough and the needle bent. She scowled and looked anxiously at her small supply. "Stand aside," she ordered, unwilling to risk damaging another precious needle.

Just outside the gate, dogs barked and yelped as if in pain, men shouted, then everything was quiet. The leader looked sternly ahead. "Other comrades are ridding the city of stray dogs," she announced. "We will make China safe. We will stop disease."

The two carriers carefully propped their banner against the wall and marched into the house to herd the rest of the missionaries outside. "What a heathen way of doing things," one recently arrived young woman said under her breath to Miss Hilary as they appeared on the veranda. I wanted to laugh in a wild sort of way: all at once, the whole thing seemed a bizarre charade.

Two other stiff brigade members escorted the reluctant children one at a time for their injections. Miss Hilary hovered near them, making encouraging comments. "There, there. Soon it'll stop hurting." Her gravelly, comforting voice settled over several wailing little girls. She dug around in her capacious bead purse until she found a clean, folded white handkerchief. "Be brave now," she said, mopping their faces. "Wonderful! Splendid!" she added as they controlled themselves.

"Are they doing this for our passports so we can leave soon?" Trevor struggled to ask.

"I don't know," Miss Hilary answered as she pulled him away from the edge of the veranda.

The brigade leader fussed with the tongs over the pan of syringes, then straightened up and with immense disgust dropped three tiny black beads onto the grass.

When the health workers were finished, Chuin-mei blew out the burner, stood, and shouted in a harsh voice, "There is work you must do. All screens must be repaired. All flies must be killed—"

"You can't kill all the—" Trevor started to call out, but Miss Hilary's hand clamped over his mouth.

Chuin-mei continued as if she hadn't heard him. "All rubbish must be collected. The cow must be cleaned properly."

Her leader nodded in frequent approval. "The comrade is right. Listen to her." The rest of the brigade nodded in agreement as they packed up their equipment.

"The dumb dumb dumbies," Benjamin grumbled. "That needle felt like a nail."

"The cow's going to go on being a cow whether they like it or not," Simeon whispered. He and I were taking turns with that messy job. "It's as clean as I—"

"Simeon!" I hissed anxiously at him.

"And you," Chuin-mei twisted her braid around her finger and turned on me. "You should organize the children and make them useful. Teach them to make this place sanitary. Many girls your age work long and hard for the good of the people. You also should do your duty. You should learn the work of the government. You should learn your duty well. The government of the people has ways to deal with those who neglect their duty," she finished ominously.

I felt bruised, as if Chuin-mei's words had been stones pelting me. This must be what she had warned me about, but why, why was she so harsh? And I felt resentful: how could I have known that this was my duty? Numbly I watched her merge into the departing brigade. I longed for good old familiar Anne.

I started inside, but Dad reached the door at the same time and held it open for me. "Looks like you've borne the brunt of it today, Ruth. It's pretty heavy sledding, but try not to take it personally."

"Thanks, Dad," I told him gratefully, touched by his effort to comfort me.

TEN

That night I dreamed I was in a huge gloomy room, holding two pans of needles, and surrounded by a circle of barking dogs. As they closed in on me, I noticed a shadowy figure behind the rest. It had Chuin-mei's pleading eyes. I shouted to her, threw my pans of needles at the dogs, and tried to run, but my feet wouldn't move. Just before they reached me, the dogs stopped and fell to the floor, dead. The shadowy figure vanished. I woke up in a clammy sweat. Dawn smudged the sky, and although I punched up my pillow and got more comfortable, I couldn't get back to sleep.

After breakfast I would have welcomed any excuse not to go to class with all those silly little kids, but I couldn't think of anything. I was the last one to squeeze onto the bench in the attic where the others were chattering and waiting. Of course, they wouldn't let me be.

Even Benjamin bothered me. "You sure look grumpy," he announced.

"And how!" Trevor chimed in.

"Why don't you hush up," I scolded.

"What's—" Benjamin began, but Mr. Hilary appeared at the door.

We scrambled to our feet. My skirt caught on the

corner of the bench and almost made me lose my balance.

"Good morning, class," Mr. Hilary said, and waited for us to answer. One of his methods for increasing our vocabulary was to have us repeat a new definition each morning, as part of the day's greeting.

"Good morning, Mr. Hilary," we chanted. "To govern is to rule, to control, to manage. The government is the group of people who govern a country." We sat back down.

I rested my head on my hands.

"Today we're looking at the government of the Manchus. What is the meaning of Manchu, Ruth? Now think." Mr. Hilary sat sideways to the table, his feet stretched in front of him.

I kept my head in my hands and stared at the floor. "Oh, I don't care about that stupid government," I was appalled to hear myself blurt out. "Anyway, why do you wear cloth shoes? None of the other missionaries wear those cloth shoes." I felt my cheeks burn. What was happening to me?

Simeon gave a shocked gasp. Next to me, Benjamin bobbed up with an amazed laugh.

"Well, Benjamin?" Mr. Hilary asked.

"Manchu means 'wonderful luck,' " Benjamin answered absently, and peered under the table. "They really are cloth shoes! What's the matter with cloth shoes?"

I stared straight ahead and huddled down on the bench. I wanted to shrink to the size of an ant. Alexandra, sitting on the other side of Benjamin, was trying to get Mr. Hilary's attention. She flapped her hand across Benjamin's face and hit my shoulder. Benjamin pushed her hand aside.

"Yes?" Mr. Hilary asked.

"They came from the north of China," Alexandra told him.

"Good girl," he said.

The classes went on for a couple of hours. Simeon, Mr. Hilary, and I took the smaller children and heard them recite their multiplication tables and say their poems. Alexandra snickered and nudged Sylvia, who was sitting next to her—they kept on and on. "What's the matter?" I finally asked, unable to see any cause for their silliness.

Alexandra cupped her hand over her mouth. "You aren't even listening!" she spluttered through her fingers.

"Why?" I asked. "What did you say?"

"I said seven 3s are 63!" She giggled.

"Oh," I exclaimed in exasperation. "Start again, then."

At long last, the welcome thump of Mr. Bowser's boots sounded in the hall. "You may go now," Mr. Hilary said, "but don't storm the stairs. Ruth, stay here."

My heart sank. I assumed he wanted me to apologize for my rude behavior, and I tried to think of some explanation, but there was none. For a while after the others left, he said nothing, letting the room grow quiet. My eyes filled with sudden tears and I dropped my head on my arms. In a minute, though, I jerked my head up and angrily wiped my face. "I'm sorry I was rude. Did you want me to stay for something else?"

Mr. Hilary put his hand on the Wordsworth book and pulled it toward him. "If you start reading, you can forget the present and be part of a totally different world," he said in his matter-of-fact voice.

I turned from him, annoyed that I had given myself

away, but at the same time amazed that he hadn't even hinted at a reprimand.

"My guess is, we'll need all the help we can lay our hands on," he continued.

"Praying and all that, you mean?" I asked unenthusiastically.

"That, too, but—"

"You make it sound dangerous," I commented in surprise, wondering what help he thought we needed and why.

"Open your eyes, girl. You're no infant," he said with rare impatience. "It is dangerous, but there's nothing we can do except wait. What I'm trying to tell you is that, in the meantime, reading can provide another world." He scraped back his chair and stood up. "I could bring only a few books with me. I'll fetch the one I had in mind for you." His cloth-sole shoes made a soft retreating sound on the stairs.

Dangerous, I thought. I knew the situation was frustrating, but I hadn't thought of it as dangerous. I wondered if anything in particular had happened.

When Mr. Hilary came back, he gave me a fat gray volume with green oblongs which bore the title *War and Peace*/Leo Tolstoy.

"It looks very long," I said doubtfully, and flipped through a few densely printed pages.

"Read Part One and see if you can stop," he suggested.

I glanced up. His bright blue eyes were gently amused. Then my thoughts swerved back to the day before. Why does Chuin-mei act so strange, I asked myself again. Why is she so warm and friendly one time, then so sharp, especially about this stupid new government? I tried to

74

phrase my question without giving away too much. "Have you ever had a friend who did and said odd things and you couldn't sort it out?" I pictured Chuin-mei's pretty smile and warm black eyes, then her scowling face and harsh words of yesterday.

Mr. Hilary laid his hand on the Wordsworth book as if to open it. I wondered if he'd forgotten me, or if he was annoyed that I hadn't shown more interest in *War and Peace*. I pulled it toward me and stood to go, wishing I'd said nothing. He looked up, his face very grave. I took a step—I was in no mood for a lecture on the value of books.

"During the last war," he began, almost reluctantly, "I had a friend, Catherine." He opened the Wordsworth book to the inscription on the flyleaf and showed it to me.

"She's the one who gave you this book?" I asked.

He nodded. "She worked with an ambulance brigade in London during the blitz. I wanted her to leave the city during the worst of the bombing. We quarreled—"

"*You* quarreled!" I exclaimed.

"Yes." He said it dully, as though it was an old, aching wound. "She refused to leave London. She said her work was the least she could do in the war effort. Before we were reconciled, she was killed."

Carefully I sat back down, watching his face.

"Keep short accounts even when you don't understand," he said.

"What do you mean?"

"Don't let misunderstandings add up. Take care of them as soon as you can." He picked at a loose gray thread hanging from his sleeve. "I know the mails are bad, but it's still worth writing to straighten things out with your friend."

I frowned, wondering whether to tell him about my new friend, Chuin-mei, but it all seemed too complicated to explain. And in any case, my difficulty shrank when compared with his grief over the stark finality of death. He had no other chance.

I cast about for some way to change the subject. "There's another thing I don't understand," I told him. "The new government. What do you think about it? Here in the present," I added, banking on his fondness for instructing us. "My parents don't tell us much."

He gave me a long look I didn't understand. "Now that your parents are trying to leave, they're in a difficult position," he said finally.

Well, so is everybody, I thought.

"As far as the government is concerned," he went on, "there are some things about this revolution that are as bad as any war."

"What revolution?" I asked.

Somewhere downstairs there was a bang of footsteps and a burst of laughter.

"This revolution China's beginning now," he explained.

"I thought they were through. Chiang Kai-shek's gone to Taiwan and the Kuomintang's been kicked out, hasn't it?"

Mr. Hilary gave a brief laugh. "Dislodging the old government is only the start," he said. "Now the real revolution gets going, and it will be brutal."

"What will?"

"Dislocating China from its ancient enduring past and thrusting it into the modern industrial present. And probably we're the scapegoats for some of the humiliations the West has heaped on China." Footsteps clattered up the stairs. "They are proud, very proud, the Chinese. And this new government is appealing to that pride in both its best and its worst sense. I only hope—"

The door crashed open and Benjamin and Trevor burst in. "Look!"

"Boys," Mr. Hilary said sternly, "that's not how you enter a room. Try again, and do it properly."

They closed the door, knocked loudly, and swung in. "Is that better?" Benjamin asked.

"Is it?" Trevor echoed.

"Slightly," Mr. Hilary said. "What did you want?"

"Look!" Benjamin flourished a partly finished cloth shoe sole. "It could be for you. Do you make your own cloth-sole shoes?"

"No. Whose is it?" There was a hint of laughter in Mr. Hilary's voice.

"We spied it on a shelf when we went outside, and we thought you'd like a new sole for your cloth-sole shoes," Benjamin explained.

"Or you could use it to swat flies," Trevor suggested amiably.

"Castor and Pollux are making mischief again," Mr. Hilary commented with a mock sigh. "Whose is it?" he asked once more.

But the boys just grinned and backed out, leaving the cloth shoe sole on the table.

I stood up to follow them. I had quite enough to think

about for the present. "Thank you, sir." Awkwardly I sidled out of the room, not knowing how to express my appreciation for all he had said.

As I went downstairs, I thought about the expression on his face when he told me my parents were in a dangerous position.

✝
1

ELEVEN

I was angry with Chuin-mei. It wasn't the almost pleasant, clear-cut anger I sometimes felt. It was complicated and uncomfortable because I couldn't forget her plea for my understanding, nor could I forget Mr. Hilary's suggestion that I straighten things out.

I stayed away from the cook's house for a couple of weeks, keeping myself busy with what she'd told me to do. However, initiating something like this was new to me. At boarding school we had responded to rules and bells in a rather mindless way, and I set out organizing the others with indifferent success. "Come on, you kids," I urged. "Here are some flyswatters and rakes. Get busy."

James, Aileen, and Sylvia grabbed the rakes and started in. The others took the flyswatters, but we were three short. "See, we can't help," Benjamin told me happily.

"Pick up the sticks that are lying around," I retorted.

He and Trevor disappeared through two ventilation holes in the foundation of the house, then wormed their way back out, bringing with them a couple of rotten wooden supports. The others were delighted, dropped their rakes and flyswatters, and followed suit. But the next day the police, on one of their inspections, put an end to that by accusing Dad of destroying the house.

They took him back to the police station for a couple of hours.

"Now what do we do?" Benjamin challenged me.

"We could dig holes and bury the junk," Trevor suggested. The rest enthusiastically agreed. A few days later the police put an end to that too, by accusing Dad of hiding things in the holes the kids had dug. Again, they took him off.

"Should we stop trying to do this stupid sanitation business?" I asked Dad when he got home the second time. "Doesn't it get you into trouble?"

He looked very uncomfortable and didn't answer right away. "Keep working at the flies and patch the screens," he said abruptly. "I'll show you how tomorrow."

The next day, we snipped screen patches and twisted the wires into the holes in the door and window screens. Then we made more flyswatters and spent time every afternoon in what turned out to be an increasingly hopeless task as the April weather grew warmer.

One day after lunch, Trevor, Benjamin, and Alexandra were conspicuously absent when the rest were dispiritedly swatting the wretched pests.

"Those kids aren't helping to kill flies," Aileen complained. The twins glanced at their sister and giggled. "This is a dumb job, being a Sanitation Brigade," Aileen whined on. "Whoever heard of killing all the flies in a place?"

"I got three! I got three!" Danny shouted excitedly. "That's sixteen now!"

"I got seventeen and a half," Ivan shouted back.

"How can you have half?" Danny asked.

"Well, it broke, and I couldn't find the rest," Ivan

explained, holding out the bowl in which he was collecting the flies.

"When will those people check whether we've killed enough?'" James gave a desultory swat and looked expectantly at me, but then focused his stare on my dress.

Crossly I fastened my button, which kept popping open. "I'll go find those three. Keep these kids at it, Sim, will you?"

He was washing the cow with brown soap and sighed loudly. "I guess."

I searched the front yard, the bedrooms, and the kitchen, where a couple of ladies were peeling and slicing carrots, but I couldn't find those three imps anywhere. Finally, in the hall, I noticed the small cupboard door under the stairs slightly ajar. Muffled laughter came through the crack, so I peered in. "There you are! What are you doing?"

"We found a fly," Benjamin explained.

"Now we have them all killed. See? Just like you told us," Trevor added. Alexandra snickered from the shadows.

"But flies don't live in dark cupboards," I said suspiciously as I opened the door wider and saw what they were up to. On a low shelf, partially covered by a piece of old sheet, lay a block of unrefined sugar about the size of a suitcase. One corner had been gouged out by their fingernails. "You silly twits. You're going to be sick. And I bet you're horribly sticky."

They just grinned at each other. "But we killed the fly!" Benjamin said.

"Come on out and get washed and then help the others," I ordered, trying to sound angry. As they came into the light, I saw that their faces were brown and sticky and very pleased.

A tiny ant struggled helplessly in the syrupy smear on Benjamin's cheek. "I like playing Sanitation Brigade," he said, and licked the smear, ant and all.

When everyone was finished and the flyswatters had been stored for the next day's efforts, I went slowly upstairs to the bedroom. Mr. Hilary's advice rang in my ears: "Don't let misunderstandings pile up." The longer I waited to see Chuin-mei, I realized, the harder it got. I pulled open the drawer next to my bed and stared at the embroidery, scarcely aware of Simeon standing nearby, fiddling with something. Slowly I pushed the drawer closed, then opened it again. Twice I did that, put my hand on my work, then slowly closed the drawer again.

"What's the matter with you?" Simeon burst out. "You never used to be moody like this. That's about the fourth time you've opened and closed that drawer."

"Nothing's the matter!" I answered angrily, and yanked the drawer open, snatched up the embroidery, and hurried downstairs and past the bamboo grove before I could change my mind again.

Chuin-mei sat just inside the open door working on a blue cloth shoe. She had once explained that everyone was making shoes for the soldiers. She put down her work. "Your embroidery," she said with a smile and held out both hands. "Show me. Is it going well?"

For a moment I was taken aback. She acted as if there had been no change, as if I had been visiting her all along as usual. "It's . . . it's no good," I stammered in confusion and unfolded the blouse.

82

"Please sit. Please sit," she said hospitably, and took the blouse. "You are learning well! Look how much better this yellow persimmon is than that red one." She threaded the needle with a fine strand of green floss. "Now I will show you how to stitch this little leaf."

My heart pounded. My mouth grew dry. But I had to know. "Why did you yell at me before?" I burst out, then clenched my teeth, afraid of her answer.

But she showed no confusion. Deftly, she put in three tiny stitches, then shook her head. "No why. No what," she told me briskly. She stitched around the point of the leaf. Her eyes looked up at me, begging. "Trust me."

I wished I could be more certain. I glanced down at the needle, then noticed that Chuin-mei's hand was covered with small bruises and a long red scratch. They represented to me that part of her life which made her so enthusiastic and which so perplexed and intrigued me. "I'll try," I answered. I took the blouse and began to work the tiny green stitches.

"The English," Chuin-mei went on cheerfully. "I've learned the body, the clothes, the street, the school. Tell me how to meet people."

I took a deep breath. She always seemed in control of the situation, comfortable and confident of her abilities. And she was fun to teach, she learned so easily. "Hello," I said.

"He-llo!" she repeated. The l's in the middle of English words still gave her trouble. I repeated the word more slowly, and Chuin-mei followed.

"How are you?"

"How are you?"

We continued for some time with other words and phrases. Then Chuin-mei said, "We are friends. How do you say that?"

I looked at her with pleased surprise and said the words. "And here is how we write it," I added. "I don't have a pencil. Come outside and I'll show you." I found a twig, crouched, and drew "O ✕ O ✕ O ✕" in the dirt.

"That means friend?" Chuin-mei asked, puzzled.

"No, it means hugs and kisses for my friend. You put it at the end of a letter." I stood up and thought, from her frown, that it must seem silly. I rubbed it out with my shoe.

"Don't," Chuin-mei said. "Maybe we could make a character like this." She hunkered down, picked up the stick, and drew: ⚭. "A Chinese–English character. Our character."

I chuckled. "Our friendship character."

She looked up at me with the twig still in her fingers. "Do you have another friend?" she asked.

"Oh, yes," I said eagerly, but I couldn't think of how to explain her. "Anne is my friend's name. She has red hair." I felt silly, as though repeating the first page of a reading book.

Chuin-mei stood up, touched her finger to her cheek in a slightly embarrassed gesture, and asked, "What do you do together?"

"She's not here. She was at my school. I'll probably never see her again."

"So you like it?" she asked shyly. "That I am your friend?"

"I like it very much," I told her.

We went back inside and I picked up my work and

84

fiddled with the needle. One question had teased me for a long time. Maybe since Chuin-mei was being so warm, I dared to ask. "What do you think about Christianity?" I said, without raising my head.

She didn't answer. I looked up and she was smiling to herself.

"Do you know anything about it?"

Chuin-mei nodded. "During the war with Japan, a kind American missionary rescued me when our village was bombed. She took care of me and about six others until our families were found. She taught us about Christianity. My relatives have taught me also." Then she shook her head. "But I don't think about it very much. My days are full with many things, other work."

"Like the river-deepening project? You must still be carrying stones." I touched one of her scraped knuckles, then went back to my leaf.

"On the days it is my turn. Tomorrow I go." She leaned toward me, frowning at the blouse. "Be careful. You are pulling that thread too tight. See how the cloth puckers?"

I took out the last few stitches. "It seems rather silly for you to carry all those—"

"You are arrogant. You look down on our efforts to improve our country," Chuin-mei said sharply.

Oh dear, I thought, here we go again. "I didn't mean it was silly work," I tried to explain. "I meant, men usually do that heavy work."

"I forget," Chuin-mei said more gently. "You are young and untaught. You haven't learned that we make no difference between men and women. All is equal. We all work together."

"Was it hard for you, being a girl under the old regime?" I asked.

She shuddered. "Not so much for me. These relatives . . ." She gestured, indicating the cook and his wife. "They have always been kind. But my mother died of the hopeless sadness."

"She killed herself?" I blurted out.

Chuin-mei shook her head. "When one is empty of hope, one is empty of life," she explained. I remembered hearing about that Oriental way of being so overwhelmed with grief that life drained out and death came fast.

"But I think only of the new ways, not the old," Chuin-mei said abruptly. "Our new government fills us with hope."

"You really love this government," I said, in slow bewilderment. I still couldn't understand how she could feel so strongly about anything as remote as a government.

Chuin-mei tossed back her braid, her black eyes shining. "I do. I do. It is bringing better times for all the people. You should, too." She picked up the cloth shoe and started to twist the needle through the heavy layers.

I sighed. "My father is American. My mother is British. But we've stayed in those countries only briefly. For most of my life, I've lived in China and have gone to a boarding school which had people from all sorts of countries. It's hard to think of loving a particular government."

"But it's your duty!" Chuin-mei said passionately, and pointed her needle at me.

"Duty's often very confusing."

"No. No. To help the people to a better life! It's clear, so clear!"

I put the blouse down. Political duty was something I'd never thought about. Even religious duty was not clear-cut to me anymore. Duty to the government would probably be just as confusing, since nothing seemed as straightforward as it had been when I was younger. I admired her uncomplicated thinking so much, but I was also vaguely frightened by it.

"Your brothers," Chuin-mei went on. "What do they think of government?"

"I don't think I've talked about it with Simeon, except for history tests." I smiled at the ludicrous picture of seriously discussing government with Benjamin. "Benjamin's too young. He doesn't think."

"You must teach him to think," she answered earnestly.

That might be interesting, I decided, but how, if I don't understand things well enough myself? I folded my work and stood up, very glad I'd come. "Goodbye for now," I said.

When I got back to the house, Simeon collided with me in the hall, knocking my blouse, thread, thimble, and scissors to the floor. "Mum's looking for you," he said enviously. "How come they always want *you*?"

"Where?" I asked, ignoring his unhappiness.

"In the kitchen."

I scooped up my things, hurried to the kitchen, and shoved my stuff onto a shelf.

Mum's face was flushed and some of her hair had come loose from its bun, as often happened when she was distracted. She handed me several sheets of blank paper, with an exasperated: "Where have you been so long?"

"So long?" I echoed. "What did you want me to do?"

"These lists," she said, showing me hers. "We have to get them done so Mr. Avery and Mr. Simpson can write the Chinese translations. They have to be done by tomorrow morning." Then she softened her words with "But I suppose we're young only once." She smiled and handed me a pencil. "Where were you?"

"I forgot you'd asked me to help," I mumbled. "I was at the cook's." I glanced across the kitchen to the woodstove, where the cook, an athletically handsome man, was adjusting the damper. He seemed to hesitate, listening.

After a while Mum said, "I know you miss Anne, but it's not a good idea for you to visit the baby too often."

I pulled open a drawer and wrote: five wooden stirring spoons, one boning knife, one potato peeler. I stared at a spiderweb trembling with a newly caught fly, in the corner of the window. My pencil slipped from my hands. Suddenly, not admitting my friendship with Chuin-mei made me feel disloyal. "I—" I began.

"Ruth!" Mum said, with a little laugh. "Get on with it. We'll never finish."

I was relieved that my attempt had failed. Good, I thought, if you haven't time to listen to me, I'm not going to bother telling you. I picked up my pencil and wrote harshly: three mixing bowls, four frying pans. "What's this?" I held up something with a long handle. "Why do we have to make these dopey lists anyway?"

"Sssh. Just write." Mum threw the cook a worried glance. "These lists are part of the government procedure to leave the country," she explained. Her hand shook a little as she went on writing.

Why is she so jumpy, I wondered. What does she think

the cook is going to do? "What's it for?" I persisted, unable to see even a grain of sense in the police knowing about our potato peelers and frying pans.

"I don't know."

For the next couple of hours we listed every item, however peculiar, which had accumulated over the years throughout the length and breadth of the cavernous kitchen. From time to time, one of the men came to collect the pages to translate them into Chinese.

"Do you think the police'll be satisfied with these, or will they come and check again?" I asked.

Mum swallowed, then frowned as if trying to decide what to say. "I don't know," she repeated.

"Does this mean we're leaving soon?" I pressed her.

She glanced at me unhappily and shook her head.

Why, I thought childishly, why doesn't she know?

十
二

TWELVE

In spite of Mum's warning, I continued to see Chuin-mei. It was easy enough to sneak off, since my parents were so busy, and pretty much left us to ourselves.

Sometimes Chuin-mei and I just sat and watched the baby, laughing over his playful ways and talking light-heartedly.

"What is it like in America?" she had once asked inquisitively. "They eat lots of candy, don't they?"

"Yes," I had answered in surprise. "How did you know?"

"In the war with Japan, when we saw American soldiers they always gave us candy."

I had smiled, recollecting the same thing.

But other times Chuin-mei was very tired and seemed to come just to bring something her aunt had asked her to buy at the market. No matter what, though, she always made me feel she was glad to see me. When I finally finished the blouse, I brought other things to embroider.

One evening in the middle of May, I saw her unexpectedly. Simeon and I were crouched conspiratorially in the corner of an upstairs veranda to watch a meeting organized to promote accusations. The mission compound was used for some of these meetings, and all Westerners were ordered to remain in the house. From indoors, Simeon and I had heard the shrill denunciations and the raucous political singing, and decided we wanted to see what was actually going on.

We peeked down on a sea of black hair and military caps bobbing about below the veranda. One man, who had a certain elegance about him, caught my attention; maybe he'd been a wealthy merchant with numerous servants a few years earlier. Distractedly, he walked back and forth along the wall, stabbing his thumb to right and left. A young boy pushed him aside and brushed paste on the wall from a bucket in his hand.

"I've never seen the yard so packed," Simeon whispered to me.

"Hey!" I gasped. "There's Dad. They aren't making *him* an enemy of the people, are they?" We shivered—Dad looked so vulnerable before this crowd.

The leader, a soldier in a tan uniform with a red armband, indistinguishable from the others, silenced the crowd with a short blast on his whistle, and signaled Dad closer to him. "You now," the man shouted harshly. "You are one of these American spies. You put up wire to trick our police. Tell us about your evil leader, this Tu-erh-man." I held my breath and made such tight fists my fingernails cut into my palms.

Dad bowed and made apologies for the poor behavior of the United States, but the soldier wasn't satisfied.

"He wars on innocent Korean peasants! What do you say about that?" He pointed to the boy with the paste bucket, who was smoothing a huge, lurid poster onto the wall: a ferocious American soldier holding a knife in one hand and a hand grenade in the other, hulked over half a dozen Korean babies lying in a row on the ground.

Dad sketched out a brief American geography lesson: the size of the United States, its large population, its many cities. "So, you see, from all this distance I do not know President Truman," he finished. "I have never even sat down to drink tea with him." Simeon and I pressed hard against the rail, straining to catch Dad's last words. "Not even one cup, so how can I know his thoughts?"

I held my breath, wondering how the leader would take this novel approach.

He blew his whistle, although the crowd was already silent in anticipation. But then he waited so long that people began to glance at each other, much too scared to even whisper or point. He blew his whistle again, and all eyes shifted forward. I froze. "I have news," the leader shouted. "There are bad Americans!"

I didn't dare look at Simeon.

The crowd jeered as their leader pointed to the poster. "But not all Americans! This man does not know Tu-erh-man. He has not even sat down to drink tea with him." Simeon and I sighed with relief. The crowd stared at Dad, and several shook their heads, perhaps in sympathy. "Do any comrades want to say anything before the American goes?"

Dad waited, then went as rigid as a man about to be struck. I peered down into the crowd, trying to figure out what he had seen. There was movement among the people near the wall before they burst into an excited murmur which grew louder as someone struggled forward.

I looked back at Dad. Even from this distance, I could tell there were drops of sweat on his face. I'd never seen him like that. I grew cold with fear. Then the jostling stopped and someone started to speak.

The leader blew his whistle. "Louder. They can't hear in that corner."

"These Americans," the voice shrilled angrily over the crowd.

I bit my knuckles to keep from shouting in shocked recognition: Chuin-mei!

"These Americans should work," she ranted. "They should not be lazy. They should ask the police for permission to find grass for their cow." Her voice grew even louder with indignation.

I've got to remember the other Chuin-mei, I thought, fighting the sensation her angry voice aroused in me.

"They should pack their baskets and always be ready to leave. They should not be lazy, especially him." She pointed accusingly at Dad.

I was puzzled to see that he looked less tense.

"The government of the people does not tolerate laziness," Chuin-mei finished. The crowd howled menacingly. Chuin-mei disappeared. The leader signaled for Dad to go. He left, head bowed.

I was confused by my friend, and felt like a moth circling a candle: fascinated and warmed by the flame, but also frequently singed.

On my way to bed that night, I stopped outside the closed living-room door where the adults were praying together. Dad's clear words caught my attention. ". . . wisdom in the care of the cow, as we are running out of places to buy grass." There was a pause and I was about to move on, but he started again. "We thank Thee indeed

93

for the cook's relative who so bravely warns us from behind the disguise of harsh criticism . . ."

I was so startled I stood there staring at the cracks of yellow light around the closed door. Bravely warns us, I thought, and started like a sleepwalker toward the stairs. He does know who she is, but then he'd probably met many of the cook's vast network of relatives who visited from time to time. Does she meet Dad somewhere and talk to him, I wondered in confusion. Is that how she knows we are leaving? No, that can't be what he means. He must mean simply these horrible public reprimands. But why does he understand what she's doing and not the police? Or can the game be played both ways? Is she perhaps giving some kind of message to the public that Dad doesn't understand? Not that, I thought painfully, please not that.

I sat on the edge of my bed, leaned down, and untied my shoelaces. Maybe she's an example of what Mum sometimes quotes: "Wise as serpents, harmless as doves." Quietly I pulled off my shoes and socks. I'd never met anyone as enigmatic as Chuin-mei.

I finished getting ready for bed, slid under the covers, and lay awake a long time, half hearing Benjamin's even breathing. "Bravely warns us," I murmured to myself.

"What?" Simeon asked drowsily.

"Nothing," I answered.

十
三

THIRTEEN

Somehow, witnessing that horrible encounter and hearing Dad's generous interpretation of it made me feel softer toward him. I still couldn't talk to him, but I found occasional jobs to do near him. One afternoon, several days later, I was in his study dusting bookshelves while he worked at his desk. Three policemen marched noisily in through the front door.

"We have come to give you orders for your cow," one said.

"I am listening," Dad answered.

"There are Westerners—the Peytons—with a compound like this one on the other side of the city." Dad nodded.

"You are to take the cow there with a sufficient escort." He went on to explain what he meant and what the duties of the escort would be. I stood stock-still, gritting my teeth to keep from laughing.

When he finished, Dad suggested mildly, "Wouldn't it be easier if one of us went and cut the grass and brought it back?"

"You will do as you are ordered," the policeman snapped. "And you will get permission from the police offices of the districts you must walk through. Now, and when you are given orders to bring the cow back."

"Shall I choose who is to go?" Dad asked.

"No," the officer said as if he'd just that minute decided something. He pulled a folded piece of paper from his pocket, spread it on the desk, and studied it, running his chipped fingernail down the list.

I held my breath, hoping I would be chosen. I was, along with Mr. Hilary, his sister, Simeon, and Benjamin.

The police left. "It sure will be nice to get out," I commented to Dad.

His face went rigid. "There's no telling when that will be," he said abruptly.

I was puzzled, then smiled as I realized his mistake. "I didn't mean out of the country, I meant out of the compound. But when will we leave?" I asked boldly. "It's been an awfully long time."

Dad frowned deeply. "There's no telling when that will be."

"Why?"

"It's too complicated to explain." He picked up his pen and started writing.

I took my dustrag and went to another room to work.

Two days later, the arrangements for transporting the cow were complete.

"Is everybody ready?" Mr. Hilary asked with his usual matter-of-fact good humor.

I had thought Benjamin would be wild with excitement, but he was so absorbed in the seriousness of his duties he hardly seemed to realize where we were off to.

"Do we have everything we need to get this cow across

the city?" Mr. Hilary asked, as if checking on picnic preparations. "The permission papers, the bucket, the mason's trowel, the broom, the lime, the—"

"The cow! You forgot the cow!" Benjamin burst out, gesticulating with the dented metal dustpan he held.

Simeon, who was more lighthearted than I'd seen him in a long time, waved the broom over his head as if it was some kind of holiday toy. We tried to coax the cow through the small pedestrian door in the gate, but she glared and stamped her front right hoof. Hastily, the gatekeeper closed the door and opened the bolts of the great gate. "Hey, boss, boss, boss. Hey, boss, boss, boss," I crooned near the cow's ear, and she plodded out onto the street through the much wider gate.

Halfway down the street, three little boys in black caps were playing marbles. They broke off their game and jeered at us: "Western imperialists! American robbers!" The cow stopped. She chewed and chewed, gazing reproachfully down at the boys as she twitched her ears and swished her tail at the flies. Mr. Hilary gave her rope a tug. Simeon chuckled and gently slapped her rump. But the cow went on chewing. "You're an independent old lady!" he said, laughing.

Miss Hilary rustled the permission papers near the cow's head. But the cow still went on chewing. The little boys bit their lips and leaned awkwardly away from the animal, which was so very much larger than themselves.

"What do we do now, Ruth?" Mr. Hilary asked. "You've been milking her."

"I *was* keeping this as a last resort for later," I explained ruefully. I dipped into the blue cotton bag I carried and held out a handful of bran. The cow started forward.

"Good thinking, Ruth," Mr. Hilary said.

I smiled and went on coaxing the cow.

"Foreign spy! Western imperialist!" the three little boys quavered.

"What were those words embroidered on their caps?" I asked as the name calling grew fainter.

"Hate America, help Korea," Mr. Hilary translated.

In the distance the same words, shouted through a megaphone, shot across the city. This was followed by a roar of voices. Most people seemed to be at a political rally; the streets were nearly empty.

America, I thought, Chicago and Aunt Ruth. "Sim, do you remember when we lived in America and Aunt Ruth took you and me and our Cousin Jane to the park with all those rides?"

He chuckled. "How could I ever forget it! We'd never seen anything like that place. And she let us go on any ride we wanted."

"And eat anything we wanted! Remember Jane couldn't believe we didn't know the name of that funny meat—"

"Hot dogs, you mean?" Simeon reminded me.

"Yes."

"And remember how she thought we should have Chinese eyes because we were born in China?"

"Yes," I said. "She sure thought we were strange. But she was nice. Remember all that fluffy candy she bought us with money she had earned taking care of people's babies."

"Did she take care of me?" Benjamin asked.

We looked at him in surprise—we didn't think he'd been listening. "She came over a few times, and we all kind of looked after you when Aunt Ruth and Mum and

Dad wanted to go to a church meeting together," I told him.

"But those rides," Simeon said wistfully. "You could even see the machinery working."

"And we went on those roller coasters and squealed and squealed because they were such scary fun." I glanced at Sim. "Have you noticed Dad still has that joke pencil Aunt Ruth gave him that day?"

"The one with the red truck floating at the end?" he asked.

"Yes."

"Remember how Jane kept wanting us to talk because we sounded so funny?" I asked.

"Yes," Simeon agreed. "Our British cousins were easier to understand. They seemed more like us."

"Mmm," I went on. "I wish we could get out of here so we could see them again. But still, it's nice being part of a family, even if we hardly ever see them. I like thinking about them."

Simeon nodded, smiling dreamily.

"Hey, look!" Benjamin burst out, pointing with his dustpan at a new traffic island down the street. It was a circular concrete slab about three feet high, with a yellow oilcloth umbrella fastened to a pole in its center. A smart young policeman with a shiny whistle leaned forward to collect our permission papers.

The cow stopped, stared up as if considering the young man's importance, lifted her tail, and made a pie. Excitedly, the man blew a short toot on his whistle and started a vigorous harangue. "The Sanitation Brigade . . . Flies bring disease . . . Can't fight the wicked Americans in Korea . . . Keep the city safe . . ." He went on for a good five minutes, while we looked earnestly up at him, thankful that he seemed to be enjoying himself.

When he was finished, Benjamin diligently scraped the mess into his dustpan. "It's all clean!" He pointed, but the mess slid off the dustpan. "Botheration!" he muttered, and started again, then emptied the mess into the bucket Mr. Hilary carried. Simeon leaned his broom against the traffic island and scattered lime over every damp patch the cow had made on the street. Then he carefully swept the white powder, twitching the broom at any lump, until it was so smooth even the young policeman was impressed.

"It is like freshly combed hair," he told Simeon admiringly, and pointed at the brush lines in the lime. Simeon smiled up at the man, who nodded and gestured us on. Miss Hilary reached to take back the permission papers and the officer gave a final enthusiastic blast on his whistle. The startled cow set off at a gallop.

Finally our procession reached the other side of the city, where Mr. Hilary banged on the gate of the Peytons' compound, shouting, "Kai mun! Kai mun!" The gate-keeper poked his solemn head through the small door. Then slowly his mouth curved in a grin which spread up his face to his bright black eyes and almost to his shiny bald head.

"Come in," he said, and led us inside. The cow stepped through the gate without any trouble. The man limped along the path as fast as his wooden leg would let him, his head bobbing up and down as he chortled to himself. When he had found Mr. Peyton, he went back to his stool by the gate and continued to watch us and chuckle.

Mr. Peyton, a lanky man with a lemon-shaped face

and a rusty thatch of hair, scowled as he listened to the peculiar order. "Why don't you sell her?" he asked.

"There's no bill of sale," Mr. Hilary explained. "Have you had any news of Miss St. Claire?"

Mr. Peyton's pale blue eyes grew icy. "Do you know the charge they trumped up?" he asked in an angry undertone.

Mr. Hilary shook his head, and Miss Hilary tried to steer Benjamin, Simeon, and me toward a spotted dog tied to a veranda post, but I moved a little nearer to Mr. Peyton to listen.

"Her cook came here yesterday and told me the police had found a shortwave radio in an old box in her attic and accused her of concealing spy equipment," Mr. Peyton said. "Then, when they got outside, she was comforting the cook's little daughter, who had cut her hand. The cook's sister arrived. I know the woman, a real troublemaker with a steam-whistle voice. She accused Miss St. Claire of injuring the child. Of course, the police confirmed that accusation, too: the child was crying. There's no telling how long Miss St. Claire will be in jail. The cook can take food to her. But after this, nobody will dare be her guarantor."

"It's a treacherous path we have to walk," Mr. Hilary commented.

"Come, David," his sister urged. "We have that long walk home with these children."

Mr. Peyton took the cow's rope and we went back out the gate.

"What's a guarantor?" I asked. But Miss Hilary didn't answer and, instead, hustled her brother along ahead of us. I didn't know what to think.

Benjamin was still full of beans, and kept darting to one side of the street or the other, to look at a chicken tethered to a doorpost, or at a couple of little girls braiding each other's hair, or at a boy making a kite. "Come on," Simeon complained after a while. "You're making us get farther and farther behind."

Benjamin acted as if he hadn't heard, then he handed his dustpan and bucket to me to carry. "Carry them yourself," Simeon told him tartly.

"It's okay," I said. "He's just little, and it is a long walk." Simeon looked disgusted but said nothing more.

Miss Hilary glanced over her shoulder to make sure we were following, and returned to her conversation with her brother. Then we heard the sharp hack of a meat cleaver on a cutting board. Benjamin grabbed my hand. "Let's look," he commanded me.

I laughed and followed him to where an old man, a street vendor, was making pork buns. To my surprise, the man smiled as we came near.

"We'll get farther behind," Simeon complained.

The old man chopped his cylinder of dough into ten lumps and rolled the pieces into small circles. Then he cupped each circle in the palm of his hand, put a spoonful of pork filling in the middle, neatly pleated the edges, and twisted them together at the top. As he finished, he put them under a damp towel. "Can I have one?" Benjamin asked me.

"They have to rise first, then he has to steam them," I told him. "Come on."

Reluctantly, Benjamin followed, grumbling and fussing about how tired he was. Simeon groused at him for fussing. Then all at once Simeon stopped. "Look, Ruth!"

he exclaimed, pointing between two houses. The evening sky had turned golden; little feathers of cloud broke off from the wide wing of gold and floated upward.

"It's nice, Sim, but we better hurry."

"When Benjamin wants you to see something, you can take all the time in the world, but if I—" He broke off and angrily stalked ahead.

✝
四

FOURTEEN

The next day Mum decided to tackle a job that now seemed really urgent, and took me with her to the luggage room to help. Over the years, luggage which missionaries were going to come back for, then couldn't, had accumulated here. Mum wanted to open everything to make sure there was nothing like the radio in Miss St. Claire's attic.

"That's strange," she commented as she opened the creaky door. "It looks as if somebody's hollowed out a path through here." Several small wicker trunks and suitcases had been untidily heaped onto the larger army footlockers, steamer trunks, and wooden crates. "Maybe someone needed an extra-large suitcase, in the vain hope of leaving!"

Vain hope, empty hope, no hope is what it is, I thought to myself.

For the most part, the job was tedious. We opened, sorted, wrote the required lists, and put things back for half the afternoon. But then, in one wicker chest, I came across a stack of photographs of Chinese women. I riffled through the collection. Most of the faces were pleasant, but none was as pretty as Chuin-mei. Under the photographs were a lavishly embroidered tablecloth and several scrolls of Scripture verses. Below these lay a dozen small cardboard boxes of exquisite filigree silver butterflies, dragons, rats, and frogs. At the bottom, carefully wrapped in tissue paper, lay a cream silk wedding dress and an Irish lace veil.

"Look at this, Mum!" I exclaimed. "Whose are these?"

Mum glanced up. "I don't know."

"Some hopeful lady," I said, and laughed.

"Or her fiancé died," she said quietly, as if remembering a particular person.

"It's funny, poking around in other people's things," I commented.

"Mmm. A little like eavesdropping on the past."

I glanced at her, suddenly aware that I hardly knew this kindly and imaginative person who was my mother.

"Ayah! Ayah! Ayah!" Mum groaned when she opened an army footlocker. "Just what I was afraid of." She lifted out several hand-drawn survey maps; photographs of soldiers, both American and Chinese; and a thick six-inch glass lens encased in an army-green metal band. She bundled up the military items, the photographs, and several other questionable odds and ends. "I'll take these to show your father," she said. "You can stop for now if you like. Some of the ladies have offered to help tomorrow."

"Why don't you give them regular jobs like you give us kids?" I asked, then laughed at the silliness of assigning tasks to adults as if they were children.

Mum sighed. "It's hard when we're all expecting to leave any day." She went out of the room, her footsteps fading down the hall.

Outside the room was a short section of veranda nobody visited because it could only be reached by struggling through the luggage in this room. I pushed open the narrow glass door to the veranda; rain thundered on the tile roof and poured down in a glinting curtain. Then I noticed something puzzling: set protectively against the wall was a short bench and a small table, and on it a blue enamel mug with half a dozen pencils and a knife for sharpening them. Beside the mug was a thick pad of paper weighted by a stone. I knew I was snooping, but I lifted the stone, picked up the pad, and started flipping through. A photograph of Mum and Dad slid out of a page covered with pencil drawings, one of Mum and several of Dad, all taken from the photograph. Then came page after page of Simeon's school friend Paul. "He is as lonely as I am," I whispered to myself.

I thought about yesterday, coming back from the Peytons', when Simeon had been jealous and angry. It used to be so different. We used to understand each other so well. I remembered a time, years ago, when our family visited the cousins in England. Mum and Dad had taken us to London to see Granny. We had waited in a long line at a crowded bus stop for one of those immense red double-deckers to come along. Pedestrians up and down the street jostled past us with packages, holding children by the wrist. When the bus came and then pulled away, there was some kind of mix-up, and Simeon and I stood alone, watching the bright taillights disappear as the bus took Mum, Dad, and Benjamin off.

I had turned to look at Simeon, and his eyes were filled with tears, though he clenched his teeth to control himself. "It's all right," I had comforted him, understanding his fear. "They'll find us." He had smiled and leaned trustingly against me.

"There they are!" he exclaimed a few minutes later, when they climbed off a bus on the other side of the street. They crossed over and praised us for staying put. Now I sighed wistfully at the recollection.

I flipped past drawings of motors to the last page. "What's he mean by this?" I fretted. My own face grinned at me from the center of the page, and in the upper left corner, a caricature of Mr. Hilary peered over the top of a book, his long black gown stretching the full length of the paper.

"Ruth, you've got a job here," Mum called from the luggage room. I closed the pad, put the photo on top, weighted them both with the stone, and went inside. The thundering of the rain grew fainter. "This." Mum held up the lens wrapped in a huge handkerchief. "Mr. Bowser says it's a naval-gun lens. You're to break it up and melt the pieces in the kitchen stove. And these maps and photos. Keep them under a layer of coal, but put them in, too."

"What will the cook think?"

"He's off today. But there's a pot of stew on the stove. If you hear anyone coming, close the stove as quietly as you can and start stirring the stew." She smiled and held out the lens. I took it and went to find a hammer and a piece of old sheet to smash the lens in, so shards wouldn't scatter.

When I was ready, I added some coal to the kitchen stove to make the fire hotter, then found a stool and sat down to put in the papers and watch. Above the kitchen was the room where we took baths in a small movable zinc tub. I could hear stealthy footsteps up there: a forbidden game of indoor hide-and-seek, I supposed. The heat of the stove made me drowsy, and I nodded off.

There was a crash in the tub, and it scraped across the floor as a scuffle began. I sat up with a start. I hope they don't make a crack in that pesky tub, I thought, it's so mended and uncomfortable already. I hunched forward on my stool, poked at the glowing red coals, and spread the glass around a bit more, but there was no way to hurry its melting. Nothing must remain, since we could not bury it; every daylight police search included checking for newly turned earth. I prodded the coal and watched, pleased to have been chosen to do something that carried this responsibility.

Footsteps! I started to close the door, but it was only one of the Goodnight Ladies, Miss Bun, carrying a glass pitcher. She was just tall enough to peer over the edge of the water crock. "Saints alive, sweet St. Ive!" she exclaimed. "It's almost gone." Awkwardly, she reached in to fill her pitcher, then hung up the ladle and, shrugging her green paisley shawl back over her shoulders, she leaned toward me. "The drinking water's finished," she whispered behind her hand in her confidential way. "You'll need to boil some more."

"All right," I said, and smiled.

Miss Bun trotted away, and the kitchen was quiet for some time.

Heavy footsteps drew nearer. I stood up, carefully shut the stove door, and began stirring the stew. An angry voice demanded, "Where is the writer of this code?"

Several policemen came in with Dad. "My daughter," Dad explained. "She wrote the letter."

I turned. One of the men held a letter I had typed to Aunt Ruth several days ago, but I couldn't imagine what code they were talking about.

"Send her with someone to the police station tomorrow," the man ordered.

"I'll bring her," Dad answered.

"No. Not the father. Someone else."

I looked in panic at Dad. "David Hilary will bring my daughter," he said in a steady, reassuring voice.

The man nodded, leaned over the stew, and sniffed appreciatively the rich smell of onions and meat. My hand tightened on the spoon as I wished them away from the stove. They stepped back and noisily opened and closed every cabinet drawer, moved several large pots and pans, peered into the crock where vinegar was being made, and finally went out, leaving a trail of muddy footprints. Dad followed after them.

I waited, stirring mechanically, to be sure they weren't coming back. My knees felt as weak as water; I hadn't realized I was so nervous. At last I sat back down and once again opened the stove, still straining to listen. More footsteps! Hurriedly I closed the little door, making more noise than I wished, and reached for the spoon. The wretched thing dropped into the stew, and I burned my fingers fishing it out.

"News, news, what's the news?" Benjamin sang out from the door. But he had a cold, so it sounded like "Nudes, nudes, whadda nudes?" Trevor pushed in beside him.

"You dopes! Why'd you come in like this? Scaring me half to death."

"Gum in like whad?" Benjamin asked in astonishment.

"Like you're the police."

"You really are nuds. I just game for my dringing wadder." He climbed on a stool and looked into the crock. "This my wadder?"

"No. It's empty. I forgot to boil it for you."

"Well, I'm thirsdy. I'll dring thad." He jumped down and pointed to a bucket of unboiled well water.

"No!" I shrieked. "You'll get sick if it isn't boiled."

Benjamin reached for the dipper, and Trevor snickered.

"No!" I shrieked again and grabbed the dipper from him, almost yanking him over. Then I flopped onto the stool, burst into tears, and covered my face with my hands.

"Whatever is going on?" I heard Simeon ask from the door.

There was a pause, then Benjamin shouted in exasperation, "Whad is the madder?"

"Oh, I don't know," I wailed into my lap. "The police came and then you scared me to death, and tomorrow I have to go to the police station for a letter I wrote and I don't know what's wrong with it. They say I wrote a code and it's plain ordinary English."

"Are you scared?" Trevor asked inquisitively.

I looked up. "Yes. No. I don't know. It's such a boring letter. What can possibly be wrong?"

"You're luggy," Benjamin said.

"Clear out, Benjamin," Simeon told him impatiently.

110

"Oh, leave him alone. He's too little to understand,"
I broke in.

Simeon gave me one look and left. I knew I'd hurt
him. Why do I keep saying the wrong things, I wondered. I stood up to get the water.

"He's just a big old boss," Benjamin grumbled.

"Oh, go away. I'll boil your water."

"You're nod very nice," Benjamin told me. "I hobe the
bolice are horrid!" Trevor snorted with laughter.

"Go on!" I ordered both of them, banging a large tin
kettle and a small saucepan of water on the stove. The
splashed drops hissed. I hung up the dipper and jerked
open the stove door. The glowing point of one chunk of
telescope lens glared at me. I shut the door and slumped
back down on the stool.

十
五

FIFTEEN

That evening Dad told me to come to his study. "What was in your letter?" he asked.

"Nothing," I said. "It was just a plain ordinary letter. It wasn't even very interesting."

Dad was quiet a while. I sat uncomfortably on the edge of my chair, while he stared at his desk, running his finger back and forth across his chin. "Well," he said at last, "when the police question you, think carefully, answer slowly, and don't be afraid to tell them when you don't know." He looked up. "When you first came, I had to write a detailed biography on each of you. They'll probably ask you some questions and check your answers against it." He frowned, then finished, "We'll be praying for you, Ruth."

"Is this a trumped-up charge?" I asked, remembering Mr. Peyton's comment about Miss St. Claire. "Will it make any difference for our getting out of the country?"

He smiled. "No. I don't think it'll come to anything," he answered with a heartiness I knew was false. "Just repeat the questions they ask and speak slowly. It'll give you time to think."

* * *

The next day, as I hesitated in front of the police station, I remembered Benjamin's sinister wish. Then a new fear snatched at me. "What if I don't understand the questions?" I asked Mr. Hilary.

He pushed open the door. "I'll explain."

"Will they let you?" I asked skeptically.

"They'll let me," he assured me.

I was doubtful, but clung to Dad's final bit of advice: "Repeat the question and speak slowly." I stepped in. The room was as bleak as on the gray December day when we'd first arrived. The only decorations were still the two portraits: Mao, with the mole on his chin, gazing serenely into the distance, and Stalin glumly eyeing us all.

"There!" A policeman directed me to a bamboo chair across the desk from a gaunt officer whose left eyelid drooped. Next to him sat a scribe ready with brush, black ink, and paper to take down what I said. Mr. Hilary was ordered to stand against the wall.

"This," the police officer said sternly. "Explain this code." He held up the troublesome letter with his left hand. His right forefinger marked the offensive code.

I swallowed, choking back a laugh which was almost a howl of relief. "Those . . ." I began. His finger slid from the pyramid of Xs and Os to a curlicue trail of them. "The X," I began again, "means a kiss, and O means a hug. For my Aunt Ruth in America."

"There!" the man squawked. "For an American spy. What is the message?"

I fixed my eyes on the little typed letters and held my breath. "That's all," I blurted out helplessly. "They just mean hugs and kisses."

"But the meaning! The message!" the officer persisted.

How could I explain something so lighthearted to someone who seemed to have as much humor as a wall of concrete.

From the school next door came the voices of children singing, "*Mao Tse-tung, Si-ta-lin, Suns in the sky, shedding light.*" They sang it five times over.

"This is the message," I said in a sudden burst of inspiration. The policeman leaned forward, his eyelid twitching. I took a deep breath. "I love my Aunt Ruth just as you love Mao Tse-tung and Stalin." I caught my breath and stared at the smudged letter, too frightened to move. My dress seemed to shrink in the heat.

The officer put the letter down and looked at the scribe covering the page with skillful brushstrokes. "Put in this also." He tapped the Xs and Os. "Why are you in China?" he shot at me.

"I . . . I was born here," I stuttered.

"Why are your parents here?"

"They're missionaries." I sat on the edge of the chair, twisting my hands and staring into the man's face.

"Why are they missionaries?" he asked angrily.

As I searched for an explanation that might make sense to him, my mind went to Granny's pleasantly crowded sitting room in London, where the same question had been asked when we had visited her. The church she went to had been bombed, so until it was rebuilt, the congregation met in people's homes. A portly woman, with a purring tiger kitten in her lap, sat near a wall. "Why are you missionaries?" she had asked my parents searchingly. It was a new question to me. I tried to remember what Mum had said that time long ago.

Slowly I answered the policeman, "In the Bible, Jesus told people to preach the Gospel to everybody and to go into the whole world. My mother and father were called by God and—"

"And politics. What politics do they preach?"

That was easy. "They don't," I told him.

"Oh?" the officer asked suspiciously. His eyelid drooped further. "Name all the places you have been."

My mouth dropped open. I looked at him in dismay; I had gone to school in so many different places. "I don't know if I can remember, but I'll try. Nansien, Loshan. I don't know all the places our school stopped at when we were going to Kalimpong in—"

"Omei. You were at Omei," the man interrupted. He was checking my answers against the life history Dad had warned me about. I recognized the blue ink he used. I leaned forward anxiously to see how long the list of characters was. "Sit back! Go on telling after Omei."

"Oh. Yes," I answered, but since Omei had been before Loshan, I grew confused and stopped to think.

"Were your parents with you in India?" he snapped.

"No," I said.

"Go on."

"Kunming," I continued nervously, knowing I hadn't included that. "Shanghai."

"Calcutta!" he interrupted again.

"Yes. I'm sorry. Calcutta. Then there were lots of places in England and America—"

"Did you go to school in America?" he asked.

"For a little while." I started twisting a button at the waist of my dress.

"What politics did they teach you?"

115

I had a sudden recollection of my first day at school in Chicago. Without warning, chairs had scraped back from desks. I had looked around in confusion to see what was happening. The children stood with their hands on their chests and mumbled. It didn't sound like the Lord's Prayer exactly, but I couldn't tell what it was. After a couple of days of this, I had asked my Cousin Jane what it was all about. I still remembered her look of incredulity at my ignorance of the Pledge of Allegiance.

"They taught us America is one united country," I answered carefully, "and God is over it."

"You lie," the police officer said sharply.

I clutched the edges of the chair.

"It is not God," he went on. "It is this evil Tu-erh-man who wars on innocent peasants in Korea. What do you think of him?"

Slowly, as if I was thinking it out for myself, I tried to repeat Dad's apology at the accusation meeting.

"Have you any Chinese friends?" he questioned.

I watched the suspicious face in front of me. I certainly wouldn't give her name to you, I thought. Aloud I told him, "Many Chinese are friendly."

He grunted as if dissatisfied, but to my relief he didn't pursue the question.

By the end of the second hour, I sagged with confusion and fatigue, hoping I'd given the right answers to his repetitious questions.

"Was it too stupid? What I said?" I asked Mr. Hilary as we walked back along the cobbled street. "I don't know much about government."

"You did well," he reassured me in a quiet, steadying voice. "Remember, the Lord of Hosts is with us."

Two boys with shoulder poles holding baskets of vegetables trotted by. "Foreign spies!" they shouted. "American robbers! Enemies of the people!"

"Do you sometimes wonder why you came to China?" I asked. "I mean, with the trouble we seem to make now?" It was so easy to talk to Mr. Hilary; he never seemed shocked or upset by my questions.

He walked on silently for a few minutes and then said, "We're answering the command of God, and that often makes trouble. And think of Christ himself: trouble whirled around him with every question he asked. But it's the kind of trouble essential to making things right."

I frowned at him. "I don't understand."

"For most of us, new ways of thinking are painful. We like water-tight schemes and regard any question that breaks into them as trouble. We're here in China so the people can choose to know God through Christ if they want to. You have to know about a thing before you can choose." He paused for a bit, then finished, "But the problems now are vastly complicated by the evils of Western business practices."

I sighed. Isn't anything simple anymore, I wondered.

We reached the gate and had to stand awhile until someone came in answer to Mr. Hilary's shouts. The gatekeeper had been dispatched by the government to some undefined duties in the country, and the missionaries took turns tending the gate and sleeping in the gatekeeper's house at night. While we waited, I tried to decide what I would tell my parents about the interview. As I was puzzling about it, I noticed out of the corner of my eye a yellow sheet pasted to the wall. "A new notice," I commented. "What's it say?"

Mr. Hilary frowned for several minutes. "I can read the characters . . . 'Ping,' " he said, staring at one character. " 'Pong.' Oh," he chuckled. "It's advertising a Ping-Pong tournament."

"What are those red circles on the street-residents list? It looks like they've just put in some more." The new ink showed brightly against the other, more faded circles.

He gave me a strange look, as if sizing me up, then answered reluctantly, "The people executed for the revolution." I must still have looked puzzled. "The enemies of the government are shot."

"But they live on this street!" I said, outraged as I thought of some of the patient faces I had seen.

"Yes," he explained. "As I told you, it will take a brutal revolution for China to move into this century." I glanced at him appalled, but at the same time flattered that he spoke to me as an equal and not as a child.

"What about us?" I asked. "Do you think we'll get out?"

The gate opened and Simeon looked through. "You were gone long enough," he said. We walked in.

"On the double!" came Mr. Bowser's command as the rest of the children pounded around the corner of the house and down the path. They jolted to a stop near us.

"Was it fun?" Trevor asked.

"Were the police horrid, were . . ." Benjamin started, but stopped abruptly, noticing I was upset. He left the line and took my hand in both his own. I stared down at his two small hands around mine. I was completely taken aback by his rare show of understanding. Briefly, I rested my other hand on his curls; it had started to shake. "They weren't so bad," I said softly. Then reluctantly I tried to gather my thoughts for Mum and Dad.

I went to the study, where Dad was working at his desk. "I'm back," I told him grudgingly. "You want me to find Mum to tell her, too?"

The relief on his face made me think of a rumply, squashed balloon suddenly filled again with air. "Praise the Lord!" he exclaimed. "Yes. I'll get her." He pushed back the chair and went to find her.

I told them, briefly, about the code and about the main questions.

"And that was all?" Dad asked.

I nodded. I didn't give much detail. I didn't want to. I assumed they'd ask Mr. Hilary about the rest.

"This means we'd better not send any more letters," Dad said. "They must be opening everything."

"Okay, I won't." I got up. "Is that all?"

They both stared at me, startled and hurt, then glanced at each other. "Don't you want to tell us more about it?" Mum asked hesitantly.

"No," I said, and walked out. I felt angry and sad and confused all at once. Here Mum and Dad had given me a chance to speak to them and, perversely, I hadn't taken it. I was in the grip of all the frustration I had felt because they didn't explain things to me. All I could think was, why should I tell *them* anything. I hurried upstairs to get my book, *War and Peace*, so that I could forget.

But I couldn't forget. I kept thinking of Mum and Dad's faces. Uncomfortably, I started to think of the many times Dad had been to the police station. Was he questioned so intensely each time? Did they try to trip him up? Did they write down all he said and then check his answers each time they questioned him? Maybe that was why Dad found it so hard to say anything. How could you explain the tone of voice, the suspicious looks that made you squirm guiltily though you had done nothing? How could you explain the sense of fear and hopelessness that such stupid questions made you feel?

SIXTEEN

The cook found a man who would sell us a daily load of hay, and the police okayed the arrangement, so in early June the cow came back from the Peytons'. That first morning, I thought I'd never get her milked. I was already irritated: Dad's reprimand still rang in my ears. He'd found me sitting on my bed after breakfast and scolded me. I had looked up guiltily because of his tone of voice, but was so absorbed in my story I hadn't heard properly. He repeated himself more crossly. "I asked what's the matter with you. Your nose is stuck in a book again, when you've got that cow to milk this morning."

I fetched the enamel bucket, put the stool near the cow, sat down, and reached for its udder. The cow sidestepped. I moved the stool and bucket after her and reached again. The cow sidestepped again.

Alexandra, Althea–Antonia, and Danny came out from the house to watch. Behind them, the kitchen door slammed. The startled cow turned, stepped on my toes, and mooed dismally. "Go on back, you kids. The cow's acting funny," I called out.

"No. We want to watch," Alexandra said pertly, and walked toward the cow. The others followed, snickering behind their hands.

Just then, two large blue cicadas started their whirring cry from the tree to which the cow was tied. Those pesty kids pointed them out to each other excitedly. "Watch out!" I yelled as the cow raised her hoof. They ran around behind the tree and peeked from either side.

"Oh, come on, boss," I whispered moodily as she let down her milk in little squirts. By the time I had half the usual amount, I was fed up and got to my feet. But I was so hot the bamboo stool stuck to me. The others tittered. Crossly I grabbed the stool, put it away, and hurried with the bucket to the kitchen.

I've got to be alone a few minutes before class starts, I thought. I made for the luggage-room veranda, straightening my old green dress as I ran up the stairs. But Simeon stood aggressively against the little table, holding his singing emperor top. He must have seen the whole thing and then heard me coming. "You've been looking at my drawings!" he said accusingly. "Nobody else knows about this place."

"So what if I looked at your drawings," I said in exasperation. I knew I was being childish but was too irked to stop myself. "You never told me not to."

"You're daft!" he answered. "How could I? How was I to know you'd be so nosy?"

I glanced around. "Where are they now?"

"I've moved them," he said defiantly. Then he smiled. "Dad asked *me* to help him." He tapped his chest with his top. "There are maps in some of the books people left on the shelves in his study, and they have to be taken out and burned. But he said I had to have something else to do in case anyone came snooping."

"So you took your drawings?"

122

"Mmm. I showed them to Dad, and he said he didn't know I could draw so well. But I had to burn the clock and motor pictures because they might cause trouble. But the—"

"What's that one of me in the middle of the page and Mr. Hilary along the edge for?" I interrupted.

"You recognized it!" he exclaimed.

"Of course. What's it for?"

Simeon's big brown eyes grew sullen. "He treats you like another teacher." His voice slid up and then down to its new low range. "You need to go back to school and be just another dumb kid."

Somewhere in the house there was a heavy thud.

I moved toward the veranda rail and was about to lean against it. "Mind!" Simeon cautioned. "That's not very strong. It wobbles." I stood still and watched a flecked brown cicada creep along a branch to a new place for its squeaky song.

"Yeah. I guess he does kind of treat me like a teacher. And . . ." I hesitated, with a further awareness of the frustration Simeon must be feeling.

"What?" he prompted.

"It must be tiresome for you."

"Mmm," he agreed, and looked away. "How come you keep going to the cook's house?" he asked curiously.

"To see the baby," I answered, taken aback.

"The way you go is funny. I'm up here a lot and I've seen you."

"I never noticed you." Uneasily, I looked across to the gap between the cow shed and the house, where he was staring.

"I like being up here where nobody sees me," he explained, "so I stay back from the edge. But I've seen you. You never saunter, you always hurry."

"I don't want to miss seeing her," I said.

"Her! I thought it was a boy."

I'd made the slip. A sudden impulse made me want to tell him about Chuin-mei. "Promise you won't tell if I let you in on something?"

"Why?"

I told him a little about Chuin-mei, and he listened with his old willingness. Maybe he hasn't changed so much after all, I thought as I watched his slightly puzzled face. Irrelevantly, I noticed a couple of pimples near his ear. "What're you thinking?"

"You should tell Dad," he told me, narrowing his eyes.

"Why should I tell Dad? She's just a . . . a nice friend." I felt my face growing hot.

"You're fibbing. Why haven't you talked about her before? Why are you always in a hurry? Why—"

"How do I know? It's just the way it's happened. There's nothing the matter."

"Then why don't you want Dad to know?"

I stared through the branches of the tree at the cow whisking flies with her tail. "I guess because he might stop me. You know they wouldn't like us being friends. But, Sim, don't you miss Paul? Don't you wish you had a friend here? You won't tell, will you?" I begged.

"I'll think about it," he said, almost as if he enjoyed being in control.

"Simeon!" I exclaimed. "You've never been like this! You've never tattled on me. Ever. Why now?"

He shrugged. There was a sly smile at the corner of his mouth which drove me crazy. I grabbed his arms, but he was stronger than I realized and pushed me down on the bench. Unexpected tears filled my eyes. I didn't want to lose Chuin-mei's friendship now. "You bean-brain!" I choked. "You won't tell, will you?"

"A big lump like you and you're—" He broke off. I looked up. His face was startled. He was staring at my too-tight dress. My face burned with embarrassment. I jerked free and opened the door. "We've got to get to class," I called back as I climbed over the trunks. "It's nearly nine."

But across the foot of the stairway to the attic lay Mr. Bowser, face down, his arms stretched over his head. Near his right hand were his handkerchief and a large box of books. A blue one, *David Livingstone: Missionary and Explorer*, had flipped onto the bottom step. Mr. Hilary, his sister, and several other people stood nearby. Two of the Goodnight Ladies hopped and fussed around Mr. Bowser.

"His back's out?" one asked the other.

"I don't know, I don't know," the second one answered.

"Yes, it is," Miss Hilary said.

"A pillow?" one asked.

"Does he want a pillow?" the other repeated as they both bent fussily over him. "Or a drink of water?"

"Or someone to lift you?"

To all of which he gave a muffled "No, Gideon's getting someone."

The rest of the children and a couple more adults from other parts of the house gathered around him. The front door opened. Several eager little boys scurried along the hall to see, put their hands over their mouths, and tittered. Mr. Hilary strode after them. "Where are your manners?" he asked in a low voice. "Stand out of the way." A spritely Chinese folk doctor came up the stairs.

Dad, looking a little harried, came up behind. "Gus," he panted. "Mr. Chen is here to help you."

From the floor, Mr. Bowser turned up one surprised eye. Mr. Chen looked as though he'd stepped from an ancient Chinese scroll. He was a little old man, bald as a peeled garlic, and very bright-eyed, with a flowing white beard. He was dressed in a long blue gown.

"I know every bone in your body," he told Mr. Bowser. "I am an old man, but I will help you with my poor knowledge and wisdom. Tell me what happened." Mr. Chen listened intently to the muffled recital. "In a few minutes, you will walk away from this step," he said.

Mr. Bowser gave a grunt like the one he gave when Benjamin assured him our marching would be correct. He seemed unable to move, let alone walk. The folk doctor knelt on Mr. Bowser's left side, looking very small beside his damp khaki bulk. He untucked the shirt, fiddled with the belt until he slid the buckle around, and unfastened it, then moved his small slender hands firmly up and down Mr. Bowser's spine.

Mr. Chen leaned forward, put his left hand on Mr. Bowser's right shoulder and his other hand on Mr. Bowser's right hip, and rolled him onto his side. His back was toward the folk doctor, who slowly and firmly pressed the shoulder toward himself and pushed the hip away, thus twisting the spine. He gave a final deft jerk. There was a slight pop. Mr. Bowser yelped and lay still.

Mr. Chen tilted back on his heels. His long beard rose and fell several times. "Get up," he ordered.

126

Mr. Bowser lay still.

"Get up! Now!"

Mr. Bowser pulled back his hands, pushed himself up, and stood looking at the kneeling folk doctor with a happily surprised smile.

"Fancy that!" the two Goodnight Ladies commented. "I never thought the Chinese could teach us anything about medicine!" one said, with her head tilted, and the other nodded in agreement.

Mr. Chen leaped gracefully to his feet and looked up at Mr. Bowser. "I will show you now what you did." He stood with his feet together and his knees stiff, then bent at the waist and put his hands on either side of the box of books. "Is that not how you lifted it?"

"Yes," Mr. Bowser said, a little sheepishly. "I do know better."

"This you must remember, or another time your back may not be so easy to heal." He moved his feet apart, bent his knees a little, and steadily lifted the heavy box with no sign of strain.

"I'll remember," Mr. Bowser dutifully told him.

That rascally lot of little boys choked back their delighted sniggers; it wasn't often they saw a teacher scolded.

Mr. Chen's brown eyes twinkled. "I am an old man of seventy-three years, but you will see what Chinese medicine does: it makes you as supple as bamboo." He bent and touched his toes, then swung backwards, with his hands arched to the floor. The tips of his fingers touched Simeon's shoes. The old man straightened, twirled on his toes, made several surprising leaps, stopped, and bowed deeply. His head almost touched his knees; his beard brushed the floor.

We clapped, and the small children broke into cheering. "Great-o!" they hollered enthusiastically.

"Can any of you men do that?" Mr. Chen asked. They all shook their heads. "Chinese medicine makes you well and keeps you in good health," he said, with great satisfaction.

The kids hurried to the landing to watch Dad escort the doctor to the gate.

"I wish *I* was that graceful," I commented.

"Mmm," Simeon agreed. "About that other—I won't tell."

I smiled at my good old brother. "You're a brick!" The relief, and the fact that he knew, made the blowup almost worth it.

When I went to see Chuin-mei that afternoon, I felt very self-conscious, knowing that Simeon could see me. I made a special point of fussing around the cow until I was absolutely sure nobody else was in the yard, then went through the bamboo grove. Wu Da-sao and the baby were gone, but Chuin-mei was there working on another pair of shoes. I greeted her, still feeling a bit awkward because of my conversation with Simeon. "Look," I said. "I want to show you what I've done." I held out the sleeve of another blouse, where I had embroidered a small jeweled cicada.

She smiled. "You have learned well," she said encouragingly.

Since the chance to be alone didn't occur often, I asked about her father, whom she had seemed so reluctant to speak of in front of Wu Da-sao.

Chuin-mei scowled and didn't say anything at first. I

was afraid I had offended her. "My father!" she said angrily. "There are many things on which we do not agree. But," she looked up, "I cannot forget that he is my father." And our conversation drifted to other things.

Chuin-mei's comment made me thoughtful: she could be angry and in some way respectful at the same time. The more I knew her, the more I admired and liked her.

十七

SEVENTEEN

By early July, our lack of enthusiasm for school was showing badly. The attic was hot even with the skylight open. The constantly deflated hope of leaving made the time stretch without end, and our attention wandered.

One day Mr. Hilary walked into the classroom without a single pencil, paper, or book. After we had given our definition of "dynasty" in a ragged chorus, and had spent even longer than usual settling down, he himself sat down without a word. He looked amused and cleared his throat. "Miss Hilary had a thought last night," he began.

We sat so still we could hear the rhythmic sound of meat being chopped in the kitchen.

Mr. Hilary went on, "She suggested we stop school for a bit and work on an entertainment. She'll be glad to help with it."

"Oh, let's!" Alexandra exclaimed.

"What a super idea!" Ivan poked James. "Don't you think so?" James's eyes twitched as he nodded.

"Can we do that poem about having the world and everything in it and what is more you'll be a man, my son?" Benjamin asked all in one breath.

"Rudyard Kipling's 'If,' " Mr. Hilary reminded him,

and smiled. I wondered if he was remembering how disgusted Benjamin had been initially at having to learn poetry. "Yes," he told Benjamin, "that would work well, with each of you taking a different 'if.' "

"Can we do 'The Blind Man and the Elephant'?" Trevor asked, not to be outdone.

"An excellent suggestion, Trevor," Mr. Hilary said.

"We'll have to find something big enough for the elephant," Benjamin announced. "Can Trevor and me ask the Goodnight Ladies for that shawl for a turban?"

Mr. Hilary frowned at them for a minute, considering. "Yes. But be polite." The two boys dashed down the stairs.

"Can we do this?" Alexandra asked. She whispered to her sisters and a couple of others, then pushed their bench under the table and knelt on the floor. Mr. Hilary watched as they began their act.

"Yes," he said doubtfully, "but I think you'd better ask Mr. Bowser to help you. We don't want any accidents."

Benjamin and Trevor came back. "She keeps praying and praying," Benjamin said.

"And she does funny things with her hands," Trevor added, demonstrating something incomprehensible with his own stubby fingers.

"Just wait a while and go again," Mr. Hilary told them. "Any other ideas? Now think."

Simeon was slouched on the bench with his head on his hand, as if watching from a comfortable distance. "You could get those kids to demonstrate the knots you showed us. They know them pretty well," he suggested.

"They'll need to know them better," Mr. Hilary said. "We don't want an Olympian tangle on our hands. Can you take care of that, Simeon?"

"I guess," he answered unenthusiastically.

I gave him a sympathetic glance, and he shrugged.

"We'll do a superb job, you'll see," Benjamin assured him. "Let's try again," he whispered to Trevor. They left.

"Simeon can spin his singing emperor," I said. "He's really good at it now."

"Can we do the daffodil poem?" Aileen begged. "I could ask my mum to unpack my yellow ribbons."

Benjamin and Trevor came back. "Now there's two of them!" Benjamin burst out.

"And one keeps writing things that look like Chinese."

Mr. Hilary frowned, unable to make sense of the boys' explanations. "Well, you can ask them some other time."

Too bad Anne isn't here, I thought. She'd have helped work up a good act. "Won't we need a stage and curtains?" I asked, beginning to get into the mood of the thing.

"What about the living room?" Simeon suggested. "The double doors would be easier than curtains."

"Good thinking." Mr. Hilary gave him a friendly nod.

Benjamin and Trevor winked at each other, then slid out the door to see again about the shawl. Mr. Hilary called them back, but they pretended not to hear.

When they returned, Benjamin said, "Now there's three of them, and that one's packing her suitcase."

"Pack, unpack, pack, unpack," Danny murmured.

"And writing Chinese things. And doing funny things with her hands and praying," Trevor added.

132

"How do you know they're praying?" Mr. Hilary asked.

"She mumbles and mumbles, but not to the others," Trevor explained. "They're in their bedroom, if you want to see. The door's open a bit."

"I think I'd best ask my sister to help," Mr. Hilary said. "The ladies may wonder what's going on outside their door." He left to find her. When he came back, he told us, "My sister says they're happy to loan the shawl on the night of the entertainment." His mouth twitched. "As for the mumbling: she's crocheting and reciting her pattern as she works. And the one who is unpacking and writing Chinese is making the required list of the contents of her suitcase."

"I thought everybody did that already," Benjamin answered.

"Pack, unpack, pack, unpack," Danny chanted.

"An order came for a new way the lists are to be written."

"Oh," Benjamin and Trevor said together.

As we worked on the production, we grew more and more pleased with ourselves. We enjoyed the focus it gave us, and the younger ones loved the secrecy. After a couple of weeks Mr. Hilary said, "Well, class, tonight's the night. I think we're as ready as we can be."

That hot evening the entire adult household crowded into the front living room. I left the excited busyness of our part of the room and went around through the hall to look at the adults. I was happy and a bit surprised to see that almost all of them had made some attempt to dress up: special clothes, pretty fans, an occasional necklace. I liked the unusual sense everyone showed of anticipating something pleasant for a change. It wouldn't last, of course, but for tonight that didn't matter. I went back around to where the rest of the kids were and watched Mr. Hilary help his sister with her last-minute coaching.

Then he said in a loud whisper, "Ready?" The banging and bumping around stopped. "Right, then. Open up."

Benjamin and Trevor slung open the doors with alarming speed, then grinned triumphantly from either side. The girls began:

> *I wandered lonely as a cloud*
> *That floats on high o'er vales and hills,*
> *When all at once I saw a crowd,*
> *A host, of golden daffodils . . .*

The words bumped along as if Miss Hilary's careful coaching to get the words to sound like something had been left upstairs in the attic. The little girls' arms, which were supposed to wave with cloudlike grace, banged each other more like branches in a storm.

As the children paused before starting the second verse, Miss Hilary's encouraging whisper came from the side: "Wonderful! Splendid! That's well done!" They glanced happily at her and finished their poem in much better style.

The adults clapped. When they stopped, we heard Miss Bun's loud whisper: "I like to hear good English poetry, don't you? It brings back my girlhood."

Next we sang the Twenty-third Psalm in Chinese, set to a haunting Oriental melody. For a few minutes, everybody sat in silence. "Why didn't they like it?" Aileen asked.

134

"They liked it so much they're not sure what to do," Miss Hilary answered in a low voice. "Look at their faces." The little girl frowned, still puzzled. "All right, Aileen," Miss Hilary prompted, "give the next title."

She took a deep breath and announced carefully: " 'If' by Rudyard Kipling." Each of us took a different 'if.'

If you can keep your head when all about you
Are losing theirs and blaming it on you . . .

The clapping at the end was vigorous.

"They liked *that* one!" Aileen exclaimed.

"Probably many of them learned it when they were in school," Miss Hilary explained.

Simeon showed his singing emperor next, spinning it so fast along the cord that the hum made one lady cover her ears.

Alexandra stepped in front of the doors and whispered to him, then announced: "Now, ladies and gentlemen, we have a demonstration of knots for your entertainment." She pulled Simeon's hand. "Here's our tree, and we're going to tie things to him."

What a good sport, I thought. His face was a funny puzzle of self-consciousness and enjoyment. The twins peeked out from either side of him, holding ropes and giggling. As Alexandra announced the knots, the children came forward and tied their ropes around Simeon, or lengthened the ropes already attached to him. "We did it without one tangle!" she concluded triumphantly. The adults laughed and clapped as if they were thoroughly enjoying themselves. Simeon hobbled out of sight to be released.

Eight children walked back on and slowly formed a pyramid. But Alexandra, who was in the middle at the bottom, giggled so hard she collapsed. Everyone else floundered to the floor. Hurriedly, they scrambled to their feet and bowed.

I reached forward and tried to grab Benjamin as he and Trevor closed the doors with a crash. As usual, I missed him, but nothing broke. Then Benjamin opened the doors again and poked his head through. Trevor gave him a little shove. "Hey! Quit that!" Benjamin whispered.

"Go on," Trevor urged, "say it."

"There'll be quite a long . . ." His head popped in. "What's that word?"

"Intermission," Trevor prompted.

Benjamin's head poked through. "Intermission, because we have to fix something." He crashed the doors shut again, just missing his own nose.

Preparations began immediately. "Set the chair over there, Simeon." Mr. Hilary pointed. "Martha? Ready?" he asked his sister.

She wore a gray slubbed cotton dress with long sleeves and a high collar. "Do we really need the blanket?" she asked. "It'll be very hot and I already look rather like an elephant."

"Come," he said. She bent, resting her hands on the back of the chair. "A little over. No. This way. A bit more."

"Stop being so finicky, David," she scolded.

"I'm not a child, Martha." He walked to the side of

the room to fetch the blanket, his handsome face slightly flushed. Simeon gave me a sly glance as if he enjoyed seeing our teacher brought down a peg. I glared at him: I hated to see Mr. Hilary humiliated, and I suspected Simeon knew it.

"I'm going to sneeze," our elephant choked. "Get my purse." Her brother brought it along with the blanket. Several tiny black beads ticked to the floor, and I knelt to pick them up with my fingernails. "Do you ever sew them back on?"

"No," she said, "I suppose the poor thing will eventually go pilgarlic."

"What's pilgarlic?"

"Bald."

"Why don't you make another one?" I asked.

"I could, I guess. But I like it. I've had it a long time." She lifted her head from the back of the chair and smiled at her brother. "David gave it to me before we left England the last time."

Mr. Hilary draped the blanket as if he hadn't heard her. Simeon and I helped attach the nose, the paper ears, and the rope tail. "Blind men get blind," he said. "The elephant's ready. And, Benjamin, put on your turban."

"The shawl?" Benjamin asked.

"Of course."

"But I don't know where the shawl is."

"I gave it to you to take care of," Mr. Hilary exclaimed in consternation.

"I did!" Benjamin answered indignantly.

"Well, where is it? Now th—"

"You want me to think, but I don't know," Benjamin interrupted.

"Well, find that shawl. Miss Bun will be vexed if anything happens to it."

Benjamin disappeared for a few minutes. When he came back, his face was creased in a frown. "The shawl is on Miss Bun!" he exploded.

"On Miss Bun! How did that happen?"

"I don't know," he answered, shaking his head.

"Miss Bun is rather forgetful," Miss Hilary said in a muffled voice from under the blanket. "She must have picked it up."

Mr. Hilary handed Benjamin his blindfold. "We'll have to do without the shawl. Get blind." Everyone moved into position. "Open up."

The laughter was almost hysterical, like the safety valve on a pressure cooker going off.

"That Martha! What a trump!"

"Can you beat that!"

"Martha and David, what a pair!"

"Saints alive, sweet St. Ive!" came a little squeak. "The shawl! I'm wearing the shawl!"

I looked out over the cheerful audience. For a moment, I wondered what Chuin-mei would have made of all this. I smiled at Benjamin, who kept pulling his blindfold down a bit to see when I was going to start, then I lifted my typed pages and began to read: "Once upon a time there were three blind men . . ."

The act went through without a hitch.

Late that night, I woke up. "David Hilary's an odd duck," Mum was saying in an undertone. "Tongue-tied with the ladies, and he seems to think he's half Chinese.

But he's done a good job keeping the children busy. Six months now."

Dad made some answer, but I was too annoyed to listen. Mum never used to be so critical, I thought. So what if Mr. Hilary wants to wear Chinese gowns and cloth shoes, that doesn't make him odd. And as for being tongue-tied with the ladies, I'd never noticed it.

They started discussing Miss Hilary in their low, careful voices. All at once, I realized I was eavesdropping on the only time they ever had alone together. Even in Dad's study, with the door closed, they couldn't be alone—people would knock and ask to come in.

I turned on my side, pulled my pillow over my ears, and tried to go back to sleep.

十八

EIGHTEEN

The morning after the performance, Mr. Hilary didn't even try to hold class. A large group had been given permission to leave, and for the first time it included several schoolchildren.

"How come they're the lucky ones?" Benjamin grumbled enviously. He and the other little boys stood in a glum group near the veranda. They looked as if they were watching a wonderful birthday party through the bars of a gate.

Alexandra, Althea–Antonia, and Sylvia, who had kicked off their shoes, giggled and skipped on the green grass. "We're going, we're going, we're going," they chanted, then ran shrieking with laughter around and around the lawn, as if they couldn't help themselves.

Aileen was somewhere in the house, crying.

As usual, the mix of people made no sense to us: Mr. Avery, the twins, and Alexandra, but not Aileen or Mrs. Avery; Mrs. Bowser and Sylvia, but not Mr. Bowser; Benjamin's Goodnight Ladies, and a couple of others who had arrived recently. The bus for this large group broke down that afternoon, and again the next frustrating day. Finally it got off, but then I felt as if the rest of us had been rejected by the police because there was something wrong with us.

I spent more time than ever reading. Sometimes I thought that if Mr. Hilary hadn't put me on to books I'd have gone scatty. I'd never needed that imaginary world at boarding school, where Anne and I had played checkers, or climbed trees, or listened to each other's gripes and enthusiasms.

By the first week in August, I was reading *War and Peace* for the second time. I loved Natasha: somehow the messes she got herself into were reassuring. My bookmark had slipped out, and as I turned the pages, trying to find my place, my mind drifted back to my own difficulties: the quarrel with Simeon and the uneasy feeling he'd jogged over my friendship with Chuin-mei. It had remained like a burr at the back of my mind.

When I'd seen her a day or two ago, she'd given me a lovely red silk bookmarker she had embroidered with a branch of plum blossoms. I had put it in the pocket of my suitcase for safekeeping. Impatiently, I turned a few more pages and thought I'd rather be like Natasha and trust too freely than be safely suspicious of everyone.

I curled up in the middle of the bed, chewing my knuckles over Natasha's plight. Several chapters later, Mum broke in on my thoughts. "Ruth," she said crossly from the door, "do come and help me. And, for goodness' sake, put down that book."

"But, Mum," I argued, "it's so exciting. They've just locked Natasha up."

"Oh, Ruth." The unusual weariness in her voice made me look up immediately. "A new party of twelve has just arrived from the hill country." She looked limp, as if all the starch had been washed out of her. "What I wouldn't give to have your old amah here right now. What a jewel she was."

An image of the kind, serious face, peppered with smallpox scars, rose in my mind. "All right, all right. I'll come," I said roughly, to cover my shame.

We made up the beds where the Goodnight Ladies had slept, and two more in the next room. "Where are the rest going to go?" I asked.

Mum sighed. "There are some children. They'll be two to a bed. I had hoped a few more could go on the veranda, but the rain makes that impossible. Miss Hilary and a couple of others are trying to fix the living room for the rest."

On the way downstairs, we met a tall, bearded man with sad gray eyes, holding a little girl by the hand. We took them to the small room with two beds. Bridget looked about two years old. She gazed solemnly around the room, then knelt, pulled her dad down beside her, and peered under one bed. "It's clean! Under the bed!" she exclaimed. "You will sleep here"—she patted the bed—"and I will sleep here," and she patted the floor. The veins showed through the pale skin on the back of her hand.

"It's been a long, hard journey," her father explained to me, tilting back on his heels. "Walking, mules, buses which kept breaking down. Nearly four weeks. Poor little mite." He stroked her corn-silk hair, which was damp from the rain. "This country is really coming apart. We had to leave my co-worker Mr. Finney behind in jail in Janlo. Something in his luggage made the police very suspicious. I hope he gets out soon, and I hope the rest

142

of the journey is easier." He paused and dropped his head as if exhausted. Then he looked up at Mum. "We're very thankful for all this, when we couldn't even send word of our coming." He gestured at the crowded bed and the camp cot.

I glanced at Mum, who smiled in surprise at the man's unusual awareness of the situation. I realized guiltily that I'd hardly been aware myself of the problems created by all the unexpected arrivals, and Mum was never one to complain.

"You ready for some supper?" Bridget's father asked the tiny girl.

"No," she said. "I want to sleep here." She squirmed under the bed and rubbed her cheek against the smooth floorboards.

"You and your sister have a bed to yourselves tonight. Come." He scooped her out and carried her to the dining room.

My mother sighed. "His wife died on the journey out," she said.

"Died! From what?" I asked.

"Meningitis."

"What about Mr. Finney? Do you think he will get out?"

Mum was quiet a long time. "I don't know," she finally answered in a sad, hopeless voice that made me shiver.

A week later, the permits came for most of the new arrivals to continue their journey. The next morning, Mum slept through breakfast, something she'd never done before. I went upstairs, stealthily eased open our bedroom door, and looked in through the crack. In a fright,

I opened the door wider. Mum lay absolutely still, her head cupped in the pillow. Chuin-mei's mother died of the hopeless sadness, I thought in a panic. I fixed my eyes on the garnet ring on her right hand, which lay across her chest. It moved. She was breathing. With a gasp of relief, I timed my own breathing to match my mother's, then pulled the door shut and tiptoed to Dad's study.

He was sitting at his desk in front of sheets of paper covered with columns of Chinese characters. Simeon sat toward the back of the large book-lined room, doing something or other. Mr. Hilary had some business to attend to, so there was no school that morning. Dad glanced up with a brief smile.

"What's the matter with Mum? Why's she still asleep?" I asked, and leaned against the desk.

He acted so strange and took so long to answer that I thought my mother must be very ill. The frown lines which were always there between his eyes deepened. His adam's apple moved up and down his neck and his lips tightened. The black fountain pen in his right hand shook a little, and a drop of ink splattered over his last character. "Matter!" he finally burst out. "You silly, selfish girl! Open your eyes. Look at all she's doing."

Simeon sat rigid.

I was bowled over. "What do you mean?"

"You keep disappearing with some book or other while she's run off her feet with extra work."

"Oh."

"She's tired," Dad went on angrily. "That's what's the matter. She's worn out. She's got too much to do. And not enough help."

144

I looked down at my scuffed shoes. "Oh," I stupidly repeated.

"And on top of all the work, it's impossible to plan. We never know who's coming or how many, or when anyone's going. We don't know the food situation or how long the money's going to hold out, or when the police will come bursting through." He was breathing fast. "So she's tired. Understand? She's tired out."

"Sorry," I mumbled, and started toward the door.

"But, Dad," Simeon broke in, "it's not just *Ruth's* fault."

I turned around. Oh, Sim, I thought, here you are sticking up for me and I don't even deserve it.

Dad picked up his propelling pencil with the red truck and held it upright between the palms of his hands. "You're right," he said after a pause. He laid the pencil on his Chinese dictionary and let his hand rest there. "Oh, Ruthie-girl," he added, calling me a name he seldom used any-more. I was taken aback by his sudden gentleness. "Everything is so uncertain. God is working his purpose out. I'm sure of that. But . . ." He made a gesture toward me. I stood tense with confusion. "Your mother is staying in bed for two days. Give her a hand when she gets up."

"Yes, Dad." I glanced at Simeon to mouth my thanks, but his head was bent. I went out, dejected by my shabby behavior, and started to close the door, but Mr. Hilary stepped in. I hurried out past him.

Later that morning, I went to the dining room to fetch a breakfast tray for Mum. I knew that was one thing I could do now. But Miss Heap, a short, puddingy person who always wore a dust-colored sleeveless pullover, was there already, listening to Miss Gustafson, a Viking warrior of a woman. They had been part of the hill-country group, but hadn't been allowed to leave with the rest. "Someone has cut all the tuberoses except the ones beaten down by the rain," she was saying. On the table between them lay a woven bamboo tray.

"Hello, dear, you're just the girl we're looking for," Miss Heap said. "What does your mother like?"

"Like?" I repeated. "Lots of things, I guess. What do you mean?"

"To eat for breakfast. We're getting some for her."

"Oh," I said, deflated. I twisted my checked skirt back into place. "I was just—"

"Aren't they pretty?" Ivan and Danny interrupted as they stumbled over the threshold, holding up fistfuls of straggly yellow chrysanthemums, still wet from the rain.

Behind them, their mother carried a little brown vase. "We're just going to get some breakfast. For your mother. What does she like?"

Dad leaned in the doorway. "What's going on? I was just going to see about something for Lillian." He noticed me. "Will you see what she'd like?"

I started along the hall, grateful to Dad for having sent me. Coffee drops and a few splotches of mud marked the way up the stairs. I reached the closed bedroom door and heard Benjamin and Trevor singing loud and triumphantly. A heavy fragrance seeped through the crack under the door.

I frowned, unsure of what was going on, and knocked. There were sounds of indistinct movement. I knocked a second time and pushed the door open. Benjamin bent grunting over Mum, struggling to tuck the top of the

146

sheet under the mattress. His brown curls tickled her ear. Trevor was crouched at the foot of the bed, making what looked like an unskilled hospital corner in the sheet.

On the floor near the suitcases stood the washstand jug filled with a huge bunch of tuberoses. Their heavy scent in the humid weather almost choked me as I stood awkwardly at the foot of the bed. "I came to see what you'd like for breakfast," I told Mum.

Benjamin straightened up with a big grin. "We already did it. See?" He made one of his royal gestures toward a tray at the end of my bed. On the plate was a pile of very wide burned crusts and the remains of a watery egg. "Trev burned the toast."

"I didn't mean to," Trevor said in an aggrieved voice.

"What about that watery egg?" I asked.

"It took too long to cook," Benjamin explained with a gesture which blandly dismissed my question.

Dad walked in. "I came to see why you didn't come back," he told me.

I turned to Dad. "Everybody's feeling guilty," I said hopelessly. "We've all turned into idiots: 'Would you like some breakfast? Would you like some breakfast?' " Suddenly I turned on Benjamin. "How did *you* know?"

"Daddy told you she was tired and understand tired out," he tossed at me, and plonked down on the end of Mum's bed. Obviously he had overheard Dad reprimanding me. I gaped.

Mum must have suspected what was going on. "Thank you, Benjamin and Trevor," she said. "Take the tray down now. Ruth, stay a minute."

"I have to finish the bed first," Benjamin objected.

"Benjamin, come!" Dad said sternly, and they left, trailed by Trevor.

Mum slid out of bed, twitching her shoulders as if something itched. "The boys mean kindly, but their help is exhausting. Would you fix the bed? It prickles with burned toast crumbs."

Mum and I both looked at the unappealing bed. I gave an uncomfortable little laugh and glanced at my mother standing beside me in her blue pajamas. Her eyes were brimming with amusement, and we both laughed, harder and harder, until we had to sit on the bed, clutching our sides. "And those tuberoses!" I gasped. "It's like that awful funeral we went to in America. Remember?"

Mum nodded and gave a few final chuckles.

We stood and I bunched up the sheets, took them onto the veranda, and shook out the burned toast crumbs, doing my best to keep the sheets from getting wet in the rain.

When I awoke the next morning, I felt as if I'd been yanked out of bed and shoved onto a gravelly road. What was that dream, I thought. What was that lovely dream? I shut my eyes again and tried to remember. Our family was in a garden. Mum sat near a very fragrant bush covered with yellow roses, and I was helping her shell something—peas, I think. Dad and Simeon were building with wood—a sandbox, maybe. Benjamin, who was a baby, climbed happily in and out as they worked. Dad was telling us something very funny, and all of us were laughing.

In class, I was very inattentive and kept trying to conjure up the dream. Once again, Mr. Hilary told me to stay behind. I wondered if he had another absorbing book to give me. As I waited for the others to leave, I watched the rain splash on the skylight.

"Ruth," Mr. Hilary said, "I'm going to take a gamble."

I frowned at him, startled.

"I think you're old enough and I trust you're discreet enough to understand some of the pressures your parents are under. I overheard part of what your father said to you yesterday."

Immediately I was overcome with a sense of guilt. I dropped my eyes and clasped my hands tight under the table.

"This country is presently in such turmoil that the directors of the mission have left it up to each of us to decide when our usefulness here is finished," he began.

"I should think that would make it easier," I said.

"Not for your parents. They have the Chinese church and all the folk they know here to consider, but they're also responsible for those of us from other missions who have to come through this city in order to leave. Your dad knows the police officers and the rules, as much as they can be known, and your mother does a magnificent job of caring for all of us here."

"Has everyone from the outstations left?" I asked. "Ages ago Dad told us that we were leaving." A drop of rain leaked through the skylight and splashed on the table.

"Deciding to leave is only the beginning. Your parents have had to advertise their intention in the newspaper."

"Whatever for?"

"So that people can bring any accusations they have against them to the police. You've heard those accusation meetings in the yard?"

I nodded my head.

"Anyone who goes to the police or makes a public accusation at those meetings shows loyalty to the present government."

"That's horrible," I said.

"Yes," he answered. "And your parents also have to find someone willing to guarantee their innocence."

"You mean like that dumb business with Miss St. Claire?"

"Exactly."

"And it's difficult to find someone?" I asked hesitatingly.

"Yes, but it's more than that," he said. "The charges that have already been brought against them were blown all out of proportion; so burdening a Chinese person with that load weighs very heavily on your parents' consciences."

"I didn't know," I said under my breath. I put my finger on the raindrop on the table and made a circle with it.

"And the whole climate of suspicion," Mr. Hilary continued, "penetrates right through all of society. Even children are praised for accusing their parents of political disloyalty."

He paused as if to decide what else to tell me, then went on, speaking even more seriously. "People ambitious to win political favor can still accuse your parents of new crimes against the government. People may be guardedly friendly or openly hostile, or they may use

150

obvious hostility as a cover for genuine friendliness, or—"

"That's the way my fr—" I started, but then stopped and looked uncertainly at him. Chuin-mei *is* different, I thought. She must be really brave to have tried to help Dad. Then I imagined her sober face when she told me about her father. I was sure she'd never publicly accuse him, even though he made her so angry.

"Go along now, Ruth. And be compassionate," he said. It seemed a curious end to the conversation.

I walked downstairs in deep thought. I was exhilarated by Mr. Hilary's confidence in me, but at the same time resentful that my parents didn't see me in the same way. Well, I thought, I'll try to pay better attention to what needs to be done. But then I went over the things Mr. Hilary had told me, and shivered. The boys' play-telephone had been exaggerated to spy equipment. Removing a few rotten supports had been inflated to wrecking the house. Those were two of the charges against Dad that I knew about, and now I understood their seriousness. What other accusations might there have been? What others might yet be made?

十
九

NINETEEN

A great deal of help was offered, but as far as I could see, Mum still did most of the work. After breakfast on the last day in August, I followed her to the upstairs veranda, where there was a bin for dirty linen. Miss Hilary, who always seemed more practical than the rest, was just coming up the back steps. "I've been hunting all over for you, Lillian. What can I do to help?"

Mum lifted the lid and gave her a rueful look. "The laundry's become a landslide," she remarked apologetically.

Miss Hilary made a sympathetic sound. "Maybe I can persuade David to let classes go for today and have everyone give a hand," she said. "Leave the whole thing to me."

"That would be lovely. It's so nice and hot today." She smiled gratefully and went back to the kitchen to do one of the many other jobs.

"Go get clean sheets and towels, Ruth, and distribute them around. Then we'll do the wash while we have the sun," Miss Hilary told me.

When all the linens were given out, I collected an armload of dirty sheets from the younger kids and took them to the laundry. It was a casually constructed outdoor shed, open on one side, where a gasoline washing machine stood all by itself. Its casters had been taken off to keep it from rolling around as it popped and rattled its way through the laundry. Miss Hilary was sorting some other linens I had brought out earlier, and Mr. Hilary was peering into the tank just over the motor, to check the fuel level. A slat of sunlight lay like a dividing line across the cement floor between them. Along the back of the shed stretched a board shelf where Simeon stood idly grating soap.

I dumped my sheets on the unsorted pile near Miss Hilary. "Did you hear?" I asked. "More exit permits today. Maybe sometime they'll get to us. I hope."

"Who?" Simeon asked in disgust, not even bothering to turn around.

"Aileen and her mum."

"Is that all?"

"I think so," I said.

"I wish we could go." Simeon turned to look at me. "Did Dad ask?"

"Hardly!" I exclaimed. "Last time he asked, they got so angry he hasn't even hinted at it since. You're the one who told me about that!"

Simeon went back to his grating, slowly pushing the block of soap up and down. "This is a stupid, stupid country," he said. "Always a war or fighting going on. Why don't they ever calm down?"

"Simeon!" Mr. Hilary's voice was stern. "There's one thing you have to remember: this country has problems you can't begin to understand."

"I know that," Simeon mumbled.

"But those problems can all—"

153

"David," Miss Hilary pleaded, "he's young."

He gave her a cold look, twisted the cap off the can of gasoline, and stood up. "But those problems can all be reduced to one factor that you *can* understand," he explained, and made an admonishing gesture toward Simeon with the gasoline cap. "There are too many people and too little food."

"Fighting doesn't help that!" Simeon argued.

Carefully Mr. Hilary tipped up the gasoline, which gurgled into the fuel tank. Then he went on: "Different factions fight about the right way to organize society so there *will* be enough food, or at least so it can be fairly divided."

"You make it sound as if, whatever China does, it's always right," Simeon answered impatiently.

"My brother has always been an ardent admirer," Miss Hilary said in a tone that suggested past arguments. She put four sheets and several pillowcases into the machine.

As I listened, I wished it was all easier to understand.

"All right, Simeon," Miss Hilary said. "Two cupfuls."

Absently he pushed the grated brown flakes into a tin cup. The weather was so hot they stuck to his hand. He scraped it against the side of the cup. "Why don't they just vote, like America or England?" he asked.

"You can't take Western ways and foist them on China. China has to govern in the Chinese way. For example, take Western independence and individualism. It would be disastrous, with so many people living so close together." Mr. Hilary screwed the cap on and put the can back in its place.

"It's already a disaster," Simeon commented gloomily.

"Do you want me to get the towels now?" I asked,

trying to divert the discussion. I could almost feel the mounting frustration. "The little kids probably have them collected."

Miss Hilary nodded slowly. But her brother took a deep breath as if to say something else, and I couldn't tear myself away. "And it will get worse before they're finished," Mr. Hilary went on.

"Is this enough soap?" Simeon held out the cup. "What'll get worse?"

"Dump that in and fill it again," Miss Hilary told him, and picked up several more pillowcases.

"The plight of the people will get worse," Mr. Hilary said deliberately. He seemed more determined than usual that Simeon understand. "The new government's very shaky. It'll be some time before they can afford any opposition. And, in the meantime, it will be jail or worse for anyone who threatens them."

The red circles around the names at the gate flashed into my mind. Then the image of Dad in front of the accusation meeting hit me. But still, the executions and the accusations were supposed to be getting rid of those who opposed the government's programs for relieving poverty. And when Chuin-mei talked so persuasively, her ideas seemed reasonable, especially when I heard Mr. Hilary's broader explanations. I had to get up the courage to ask Chuin-mei more specific questions, but I didn't want to make her upset with me.

"This doesn't mean I support all they're doing," Mr. Hilary said suddenly, as if to address Simeon's earlier remark. "But you do need to understand why they're doing it, before you criticize them."

Miss Hilary dropped the pillowcases in the washing

machine. "The hot water, David. You can fetch it now," she said firmly, and distributed the soap chips around a little more evenly.

"They're a splendid people with a nearly impossible task. Remember that, Simeon and Ruth," he said as he picked up two wooden buckets and went to the kitchen.

"What a mixed lot we are," Miss Hilary commented, apparently to the washing machine.

"The four of us?" Simeon asked, puzzled. He trickled another cup of the brown soap chips into the machine.

"All of us in this household," she explained. "As far as that goes, all of us in this country, both Westerners and Chinese." She was quiet for a minute, then went on, as if quoting from something she had read, and speaking almost to herself. "But we and they are all caught in the bundle of life." She lifted her head and looked at Simeon. "And what a bundle it is!" She gave a low, astonished chuckle.

A couple of days later, the weather had shifted again. I watched the dark, churning clouds which matched my mood—I'd been thinking about my parents' difficulties and the problems connected with getting out of the country. I decided to get my embroidery and see if Chuin-mei was at the cook's house. As I walked down to the bamboo grove, several missionaries were kneeling beside the well, making some kind of repairs on the pump. They were talking and laughing among themselves, oblivious of my passing. The leaves hissed in a sudden breeze. The door of the little house stood open. Wu Da-sao was nowhere in sight. I paused a minute and smiled to see Chuin-mei touching the baby's face, saying the English names in a singsong way which made him laugh and reach for her finger.

I sat down with the pillowcase I'd been working on in my lap, and we made small talk for a while. Then, hesitantly, I asked, "You know that list at the gate?"

Chuin-mei nodded.

"Well, did you *know* they're killing people?"

"Yes, just the same as war. Or America in Korea," she answered promptly.

"But some of them live on this very street! Plain, ordinary people!" I paused. "Like us!" I added as a startled afterthought.

"Sssh. I don't order their death. But if it has to be . . ." Chuin-mei shrugged in a gesture of acceptance. "It is all part of making our country equal. Those who oppose the good work must go. They are few. The people benefit." She stroked the silky black hair of the baby in her lap, then blew down his neck. He squirmed happily.

"But . . ." I was outraged: she sounded as if she was talking about wooden dolls. " 'The people,' you say. 'The people'—" In my excitement I dropped my embroidery. "You are so vague and general—"

"You are so patronizing!" she said.

"Yes," I replied meekly, abruptly aware of how much older she was than my fourteen years. I picked up the pillowcase, brushed it off, and folded it on my lap. "I don't mean to be patronizing—Mr. Hilary told me that once too. I'll see if I can remember what he explained to help me understand better." I leaned forward, put my elbows on my knees and my head in my hands, then spoke slowly, staring at the floor. "He said it staggers the imagination to think of bringing this nation forward

157

into the twentieth century. He said we have to understand what is happening from the perspective of what is being attempted." I tried to remember exactly the things he had listed. "Reorganizing the whole society and land more justly; modernizing agriculture, and industry and health care—"

The baby had been sitting like a small, genial Buddha, but now he began to whimper. I picked up a palm-leaf fan from the floor and waved it slowly in front of him. He grabbed it. I got up to find another. "I've never been around someone involved in politics, Chuin-mei," I told her shyly. I sat down again and waved the new fan to cool the baby.

"It's the only life!" Chuin-mei said urgently. She gave her braid an excited toss, a gesture I had come to recognize. The red yarn which held her black hair slipped to the floor. "It's the first time the peasants and the women have told the government what to do. We must all struggle. We must all struggle against the old ways. We must struggle to bring in the new ways of the 'five loves'—"

"The five loves? What's that?"

Chuin-mei held up the baby's hand and raised one chubby little finger for each item. "Love of the fatherland, love of the people." He watched and gurgled happily. "Love of labor, love of science, love of public property."

Into my mind came the ludicrous picture of a new Mother Goose: This little pig loves the fatherland, this little pig loves the people . . .

Chuin-mei looked at me with a quizzical expression on her face. "What do girls in America do?" she asked.

"Little girls, you mean?" I countered, not understanding her question.

158

"No," she said. "Young women like me."

I frowned, trying to think. "I guess they mostly become teachers or nurses or secretaries, or get married."

Chuin-mei looked very pleased. "You see? Even American girls can only do some things. We are changing all that. In old China, girls were worth nothing. In new China, we can do all the work men do!"

"I have a cousin in America I haven't seen for a long time," I told Chuin-mei, "and she says all she wants to do is grow up, get married, and have lots of babies."

The baby hit his fan against the one I was still waving in front of him. He laughed and started to crow with pleasure.

"If her babies are all like this one, she will be fortunate," Chuin-mei said. She watched him for a minute, then asked, "In America, do they play with their babies?"

"Probably," I said. "But I've hardly seen any Americans with their babies."

As I walked up the path, I felt thoroughly content, as though at last the penny had dropped. I realized that Chuin-mei's irritation was something that flared and died equally fast, that she really was very warm and friendly.

二十

TWENTY

When I got back to the house, the smell of onions cooking reminded me that I was supposed to be helping make supper. Anxiously, I hurried to the kitchen.

Mum sat on a stool chopping carrots, since the cook was away at a political rally. A big bowl of bread dough I had seen Trevor's mother mixing up earlier was near her hand. Mum glanced up. "Where have you been so long?" she asked.

"Playing with the cook's baby," I told her.

"Who else is out there?"

I laid my embroidery on a shelf, stalling for time. "The cook's relative," I finally said. "I didn't realize I'd been gone so long."

She looked up at me with a worried frown. "What do you talk about?" she asked.

I shrugged. "Embroidery, babies, government, America, and I've been teaching her English."

Mum flinched as if my words were wasps in her ears. "You've been *what*?"

"She wants to learn English. And she's teaching me to embroider." I went and got my work and spread it out for Mum to see, but she barely glanced at it.

"What kind of English?" she asked.

"English English. What do you mean?"

"What sorts of phrases?" she asked, not relaxing one bit. The worry on her usually gentle face was deepening.

"Ordinary conversation, travel, places. That sort of thing."

Mum said nothing.

"She learns really easily," I added quickly. I watched my mother dice the carrots smaller and smaller. "You'll cut your fingers. What are you doing with those carrots?" I asked, hoping to change the subject.

"Oh," Mum said absently, and pushed them from the cutting board into a pot. She slit open a green pepper and started to take out the seeds. "Ruth, you must not visit that girl again." She pinched off the words.

For a moment I stared, too stunned to say anything. Then I asked, "But why not?"

"The political situation is so uncertain. You never know who may be an informer, and there's something peculiar about her wanting to learn English." She raised her head and gave me a long look I didn't want to understand.

"Oh, Mother!" I said in frustration. "Why do you have to be so suspicious!"

Mum stabbed the knife into the cutting board. "This country's gone crazy. Everything's topsy-turvy. Do you want to jeopardize our chances of getting out?"

"But Chuin-mei. She's . . ." I started. "She's wonderful. And anyway, she's given us warnings before. I heard Dad pray about it. Why—"

"Ruth!" Mum interrupted. "Things are so confused we simply can't take any chances if we want to leave."

161

I opened my mouth to object.

"Never visit her again." Her voice was as hard as granite. "Chop those peppers and that cabbage."

"Are you going to forbid her to come here?" I asked.

"You know I can't do that." Mum stood up abruptly and went out.

I was so angry and upset that I jerked the knife from the board and cut my palm, then started chopping the green pepper and cut my thumb. I shoved the curved strips off the board into the pot, leaving a messy red streak. "Oh, I hate this stupid life! I hate it! I hate it!" I said furiously.

After supper, Simeon and I squeezed into our concealed place to watch an accusation meeting. Several soldiers made their way to the front of the crowd, carrying a large banner of anti-American slogans. In the far corner of the yard, three men in pointed paper hats stood with heads bowed, their hands on their knees, in an attitude of deep shame.

"Why are we watching, anyway?" I mumbled.

"There's nothing else to do." Simeon pointed to a group of girls singing: *American robbers, come to harm us . . .* "Isn't that the girl who yelled at Dad about the cow? Is she the friend you told me about?"

"I guess," I mumbled and squirmed backwards. I was still angry with my mother, but I also realized I wasn't up to one of Chuin-mei's shrill accusations either, if that's why she was here. "I'm going in. I don't want to watch," I told Simeon.

He stared at me. "What's the matter?" he asked slowly. "You're acting so funny today."

I shrugged and headed for our bedroom. As I passed

one closed door, I heard, "That awful political singing. It haunts you like a nightmare."

"The poor poor Chinese," someone answered.

At the end of the hall, I found Benjamin wearing a tall pointed paper hat. He tottered up to Trevor, who had his glasses pushed to the end of his nose as if he was an old man. "Oh, dear comrade," Benjamin quavered, "I have too much land. I am ashamed. Please take it from me."

"The Land Reform is progressing," Trevor intoned in a pompous voice. He knocked Benjamin's hat off.

"You idiots!" I said angrily. "Haven't you any idea how horrible it all is? Can't you find something more sensible to do?"

"What's the matter with *her*?" Trevor whispered.

"She thinks she's turning into a grownup!" Benjamin said in disgust.

I slammed into the bedroom and flopped on my bed. "Why? Why? Why?" I whispered fiercely into my pillow. At the back of my mind was something I didn't want to face, but I wasn't sure what it was.

二十一

TWENTY-ONE

I stayed away from the cook's house for the next three weeks, three horrible weeks when the things Mum had said, the comments Mr. Hilary had made, the urgent explanations Chuin-mei had given, all taunted me. War, political executions, revolutions, uprisings, the inequality of wealth and poverty: all these things tangled in my mind. But none of them could match the gnawing sense that maybe I was trusting Chuin-mei foolishly. Yet, when I pictured her eager, interested face, I felt that any suspicion was stupid, really stupid. But why *did* she talk so much about politics? Why *did* she ask my opinions? Why *did* she want to learn English, as Mum had said. Wu Da-sao had been unhappy with my visits from the start, and I had assumed that was because it was not customary. But maybe there were other reasons.

Early one sultry gray afternoon toward the end of September, I sat on my bed reading. Simeon was on his bed, drawing a vase he had set on a tray beside him. "You know what I saw on Dad's desk?" he asked after a while.

"No. What?" I answered, but went on reading.

"Underneath that glass top—"

I looked up. "You can't ever see there," I interrupted. "It's always covered with papers."

"There are photos of all of us. As babies!"

"On Dad's desk!" I exclaimed.

"Yes. I saw them." Carefully, Simeon shaded the edge of the vase he was drawing.

"He probably wishes we were all still babies," I commented irritably. "I'm glad Mr. Hilary—"

"What's that?" Simeon broke in.

We frowned at each other. Bedroom doors down the hall were being noisily opened and slammed shut, footsteps banged nearer.

A young police officer, no more than fifteen or sixteen years old, glared in at us. We froze. He looked cautiously around the room, then walked over to Simeon and gazed at his drawing of the vase with a single tuberose in it. I breathed more easily as I saw the interest in his face. "You draw very well," he told Simeon admiringly.

Simeon gave him a surprised smile.

"I used to draw at my home near Kweiyang." The policeman named a place well to the south, and his voice was wistful. "I drew our peony bush, and our chickens, and our pig, and once my little brother."

"You're very far from your family," Simeon said.

The boy nodded unhappily.

"Would you like to draw something now?" Simeon flipped a page and held up the pencil.

The young man looked longingly at the pencil and reached for it. Clipped footsteps sounded in the hall downstairs. Immediately his expression changed. "Follow me!" he commanded.

165

Quickly we put our things aside and hurried after him into the hall.

"Take everything out. Everything!" he shouted harshly, opening the linen cupboard.

Simeon emptied the shelves, handing things to me. I was thankful this was such a safe cupboard, unlike the trunks, where anything might turn up. I piled the sheets, towels, and pillowcases along the hall floor, propping them against the wall so they wouldn't spill over.

When the shelves were empty, the young officer leaned down and pointed. "Try down there. See if there is more," he told us. We knelt, peered way under the bottom shelf of the cupboard, and pulled out a couple of small baskets I hadn't known were there. One by one we held things up: several spools of thread, a few half-hemmed table napkins, and other odds and ends.

Several more policemen came up the stairs, with Dad following behind them. "Have you taken out every-thing?" the leader asked. He was the one with thick glasses who had come the most frequently. He frowned at the uninteresting piles of towels and bed linens. The boy nodded. "You found nothing?" He spread his hands.

I glanced at the new group. I was so startled I dropped the three spools of thread from my hand, and they rolled noisily across the floor. I gritted my teeth and looked back down, breathing quickly. The expression on Chuin-mei's face made me feel like a traitor. She looks hurt or puzzled, I thought. I absolutely have to see her again so I can explain. I reached for the scarlet thread, which had rolled against her foot. We glanced swiftly at each other, and I made as much of a smile as I dared.

"What about that dark top shelf?" the leader asked.

Shakily I got up, ran my fingers across the board, and showed him the dust on them. "There's nothing," I said.

But the young officer, exhibiting his enthusiastic willingness, braced himself on the second wobbly shelf and felt around the top, empty board. He reached far to the back, let out an excited gasp, and pulled out two dusty Second World War mosquito bombs. They were army green, with the directions on them in white. The leader looked interested and took one. "What are these?"

"You push that little button and spray it," I explained.

Dad chuckled. "It's for mosquitoes."

The man turned it over and over in his hands, wiping off the dust with his thumbs.

"It's all right," Dad told him. "They're not atom bombs."

The leader's black eyes flashed. I could see he found Dad's comment anything but amusing. He opened his mouth to shout, but just then the young officer jumped down. "And see!" he announced. Triumphantly he held up an army chocolate can that held two tiny rubber dolls, a Ping-Pong ball, and half a dozen bullet shells.

My knees grew so weak I almost sat down on the pile of sheets.

The man broke into a violent harangue about trickery, vicious Western spy techniques, American ill will and brutality in using the atom bomb. "And now where is the gun?"

Simeon gave a frightened gasp.

"Gun?" Dad repeated in a puzzled voice. "There is no gun."

"You lie," the officer spat at him. "There are the cartridges. Bring out the gun."

Quietly Dad explained, "Those are from some child's

167

collection years ago." He took one of the tarnished shells and examined it. "I didn't even know they were there."

"It is your duty to know what is in your house. Jail! You will come with me to jail for keeping suspicious weapons!"

Dad held up the small, old shell. "For this!" he said. But they led him away.

I swallowed to hold back the tears. What would they do to him? I looked at Simeon; he was white. "Come on," I said. "Let's follow." I pulled him after me to watch Dad as long as we could. We went outside, and stepped over the threshold of the compound gate.

"Stay inside," barked the leader.

We stepped back in, pulled the gate closed, but left a crack wide enough to see until Dad and the men disappeared.

"Did you see who was with them?" Simeon asked me accusingly, as we went to find Mum.

I said nothing, too stunned by what had happened to think clearly. But later, as I went over the scene in my mind, I thought, No! No! Simeon's wrong. I don't understand what's happened, but he must be wrong.

That evening I helped Mum fill a basket of food for Dad, since the families of prisoners were required to feed them. "Isn't this enough?" I asked after I'd made four peanut-butter sandwiches.

"If I know your father, he'll give most of it away. Some of those families can't send food in very often." She passed a piece of chicken to me. "Slice that as thin as you can and make four more."

"How will the cook know which prison Dad's in?"

"He'll have to ask at the police station. I hope they don't send him on a wild-goose chase."

"Are you . . ." I started and gave her a sideways glance. "Are you scared?" I hardly dared breathe as I waited for her answer, stealthily watching her face. Her eyes filled with tears and she nodded as if she didn't trust herself to speak.

The cook came in, saw what we were doing, and put a kettle of water on the stove to make a thermos of tea. When it was ready, he left. A couple of hours later, he returned. "He is at the main prison, the one which was a temple," he told us.

"Did you speak with him?" Mum asked eagerly.

"No," the cook answered. "I gave the food to the guard. He said he would get it to him."

That night I fell asleep right away, but later on woke up and looked over toward my parents' bed. I couldn't see anyone. I sat up. The bed was empty. I pulled my knees up, wrapped my arms around them, and put my head down on them. Do I dare look for Mum to try to comfort her, I wondered. I wouldn't know what to say. Nothing seemed appropriate. Then a thought chilled me, as if a gun barrel had slid down my back: that jail may be the last place Dad sees. And that sight Simeon and I had of him walking down the street between the guards may be the last. I heard the faint sound of someone walking barefoot up the stairs, coming toward our room. Quickly I lay down and feigned sleep.

One afternoon a few days later, I was sitting on the upstairs back veranda watching Trevor and Benjamin blow bubbles. Mum had told Benjamin that Dad was off on a trip, and his ignorance and consequent unconcern were comforting.

The two little boys had wooden spools and bowls of soapy water. "Botheration! I can't do it," Benjamin complained after a while. "Show me, Trev."

"You blow too hard. Watch. Like this." Trevor put the soapy spool to his mouth and blew very gently. A stream of tiny bubbles, then a large one, escaped from the hole.

"There!" Benjamin said excitedly as his first bubble floated up. "It worked! Look! The tree's turning mine green!"

"The sky's making mine silver!" Trevor pointed up.

"Mine's going highest of all! It's almost over the roof. Look! Look!" I watched Benjamin's shining bubble rise. "Oh, it popped." He dipped his spool in his bowl. "Don't you wish we could have gone away on the bus with Danny and Ivan and James? I wonder when *we* get to go."

"Probably you get to go with their dad and I get to—"

Simeon banged through the hall door. He seemed unable to settle down and turned up all over the house when he wasn't brooding on his bed. "Why did you dopes go off and leave me?" he asked crossly. "You said you were bored because everybody's left, so I was nice enough to show you my special veranda. I thought you were coming back."

"We just wanted to do bubbles!" Benjamin answered indignantly, and sent a few more floating up.

"What are they doing this time?" Trevor whispered.

"Who?" Benjamin whispered back. "Why are you whispering?"

I got up and moved carefully toward the rail to see what they were talking about.

Below us, at the well, Mr. Hilary and a couple of other men with screwdrivers and hammers were crouched around the pump, taking it off its platform. Miss Heap and Miss Gustafson looked on anxiously. Beside them stood half a dozen policemen with ropes and a large wooden bucket.

"You'd think those police live here, they come so much now," Simeon said.

"Maybe they're still trying to find the guns they've been yelling about," Benjamin suggested.

"In the well?" Simeon asked.

"That is a funny place," Benjamin admitted.

After the pump and its long piece of bamboo piping were removed, the police lowered the empty bucket into the black mouth of the well, then stopped. A skinny little man with a flashlight and a mason's trowel stepped down into the bucket.

Hand over hand, the policemen slowly lowered the rope, until there was a splash and a hollow call from the well. One man knelt at the edge and shouted instructions into the darkness. Thin, incomprehensible sounds came back up. Then the men started hauling the bucket up, shouting angrily at each other. The small man stepped out of the bucket, still holding the flashlight and trowel. One man left the group and hunted about until he found a long bamboo pole with an iron hook on the end. He was let down with the pole, but came back up with nothing, just like the first fellow. "No gun!" he exclaimed irritably. "There was no gun."

"They act as if finding nothing makes them think we're hiding something. I wonder how you're supposed to show you're innocent," Simeon said gloomily.

"That is the way it seems," I agreed.

"They're just dopes," Benjamin commented, sending a stream of bubbles floating out over the policemen's heads.

二十二

TWENTY-TWO

As the days of Dad's imprisonment went by, the seventh day, the eighth day, the ninth day, our hopes grew smaller and smaller. I thought often of Chuin-mei, too, and wondered if she knew anything about Dad.

We couldn't be sure he was getting the food we sent, since the cook saw only the guard. But the cook did say that several of the Chinese church folk had walked past the jail when the gate was open, and that they had seen Dad sitting on one of the board shelves where the prisoners were kept. So at least we knew he was still alive.

I wondered how Mum could be so strong, so undaunted by the circumstances. She was very subdued, but she did all her usual work. "How can you go on?" I asked her as we folded bed sheets together one afternoon.

She gave a broken little laugh. "God has given us the gift of hope for times like this. If . . . if something worse happens, God will give the strength for that when that time comes. We don't need to borrow trouble from tomorrow."

She so seldom said anything about what she thought, or why she acted as she did, that I was very moved. "Thanks, Mum," I said. She gave me one of her rare hugs and quickly picked up another sheet to fold it.

On the tenth night, I went to bed and dreamed I was in a gloomy locked room with dark dogs sniffing and snarling about. I couldn't find the door to get out, but I knew Chuin-mei was somewhere outside trying to help me, banging on the wall to make a hole. I sat up in bed, half awake, straining to hear. There really was pounding downstairs on the front door. Then, instead of the usual angry police voices, I heard, "Thank God!"

"Praise the Lord!"

"You're back!"

Simeon asked sleepily, "What's all the racket?"

"I think Dad's back."

"You mean it?" He slid out of bed, and together we went down the stairs.

"That's Dad?" I whispered to Simeon.

Dad stood just inside the front door, and beside him Mr. Bowser, whose turn it was to sleep at the gate. Mum and several others in pajamas squinted at them by the beam of a wavery flashlight.

"I'll tell you about it tomorrow," Dad said. "Right now I'd need nails to hold my eyes open. I've been questioned day and night." I could hardly believe it was Dad. In the poor light he was scarcely recognizable, with his hollow cheeks, matted hair, ten-day whiskers, and unkempt clothing. He smelled foul.

Dad slept round the clock. When he finally woke up, late on the second morning, he did tell us some things, but slid over most of the experience in a way that tantalized me.

When I pressed him to tell me more, he answered, "Be thankful it's over, Ruth." That night, long after Benjamin and Simeon had gone to sleep, I lay in the dark, thinking and listening. I could hear footsteps on the stairs and fading down the halls, door after door closing. Mum called out to some final person who came up, but then *her* footsteps continued on to the study. My heart pounded and my breathing grew faster as I decided what to do.

I pictured the closet next to the study where chairs were stored. It had a thin partition at the back, and once, when I'd been putting away a chair, I'd overheard Dad reprimanding Benjamin on the other side. Stealthily, I crept downstairs, made my way to the back of the closet, and pressed my ear to the wall. Mum was murmuring something.

Then Dad's voice burst out as if he was relieved to tell her what had happened. "I've gone over it so many times, but I don't know what came over me, to make that foolish joke about that mosquito bomb not being an atom bomb.

"The police took me to the main prison, you know, the one that was a temple. The heavy black gates are the same, but it's strange to see prison guards with bayonets outside it now, instead of those crowds of beggars. The escort and guards argued for some time about which jail I should be taken to. Finally they led me into a small room, where that boy officer stood and watched while a prison official frisked me: hair, loose shoe sole, and all. They didn't find a thing except that pencil from my sister, which made them very suspicious. I hated to give it up. Silly, isn't it, how something like that is so precious because of the person who gave it to you.

"They kept it and shoved me on into another room, where an older officer sat with a scribe beside him. He went through the usual routine of 'Where were you born?'

and 'What is your work?' until, I suppose, he thought he had me lulled. Then he snapped, 'Where is the gun?'

"I told them there was no gun. There never had been a gun.

" 'You had cartridges,' he accused. 'There must be a gun.'

"It was a triple crime: having cartridges, lying about them, and owning two bombs." Dad sighed. "For the crimes, they had a big black register." He gave a low chuckle. "There was a glossy black beetle, about the size of the scribe's fingernail, which crept to the middle of the page, as if it was trying to see what the evil American had done. It was shut into the book."

In the closet, I rubbed the bridge of my nose to keep from sneezing.

"The questions went on so long it grew dark and a boy brought in a lamp and set it on the corner of the desk," Dad continued. "The flame threw the officer's shadow across those awful portraits of Mao Tse-tung and Stalin. When he finally finished his questioning, he snapped, 'You are number 71. You will not speak. You will not walk. You will sit until your number is called.' The young officer took me away to the courtyard. It was uncanny, but I could feel more than see that the space was packed with people. 'Here,' the young fellow ordered me. 'Climb to your place with the men.' I slid my feet carefully over that stone pavement so I wouldn't step on anybody.

"I heard the soft sound of people shifting to make room for me; and now that the guard couldn't see them, they reached out to guide me to my place three levels up.

"The toilet bucket must have been very full, because

the stench was overpowering. All night long, the guard padded around the courtyard. The only time he stopped was when someone called for permission to use the bucket. I slept on and off. I'm so much taller than the other prisoners, I woke up once to find my cheek resting on a snoring head.

"Just before dawn, a voice shouted, 'Seventy-one, come down.'

"I was very stiff and in that dirty light I didn't notice a loose paving stone. That wretched shoe sole caught in the crack and threw me against the guard. 'Western dog! Walk straight!' he shouted at me.

"And then the routine started over again. 'Give us your gun, or you know what will happen.'

"It was hopeless. I just kept repeating, 'There is no gun. I tell you the truth.' The questioning went on day and night. I lost track of time." Dad stopped and Mum asked some question.

"That was the most amazing thing of all," Dad said. "Sometimes in the afternoons the guards left the gate open. Usually the street outside was empty. But one afternoon there was a crowd, a surprisingly large one, of men and women walking silently past the gate. There were no banners, no shouted slogans. As I looked, I thought I must be dreaming, because the faces were familiar: Pastor Chen, dear Miss Lin, old carpenter Liu, Miss Wang the Bible woman, and others. They—"

"All from church!" Mum interrupted.

"Yes," Dad said. "They didn't look in the gate, or make any sign of recognition. Three times they passed. And the next day they did it again. It gives me the chills every time I think of the courage of those folk, daring that protest for me, braving their lives for a prisoner of Jesus Christ.

"That afternoon," he went on after a bit, "the interrogation did change. 'Just hand over your gun and all will be forgiven.' But I still had no gun. When I got back to my place that time, my snoring fellow prisoner was gone. There had been one of those terrible truckloads taken out for execution that day."

"Those poor folk," Mum groaned.

Dad continued, "His place had been taken by a ragged little man whose terror was so abject he didn't even look up when I got to my place. He just sat hunched over with his arms around his knees, whimpering. So many of them seem more like hunted animals than like people. I thought of Christ's words, 'I am with you always.' It helped to pray for those folk."

Dad was quiet for so long that I thought he had finished. I started to back out past the chairs. But then he added, "And in the middle of the night they freed me, with no explanation."

Mum asked something.

"Nobody's heard anything of her," Dad answered. He prayed, thanking God for his own safety and asking for Miss St. Claire's and then naming their Chinese friends as well.

Very carefully I made my way out of the closet and to bed. As I went over what Dad had said, I realized he had shown no bitterness. I couldn't help but admire him. Yet, in some crazy way, I felt hollow and distant when I thought of him as my father. Couldn't he see that I was growing up, that I could have understood his imprisonment, too? He used to tell us things that happened, at least I thought he did, when we were traveling around England and America. But now—I knew my irritation was unreasonable, that the situations were different. Even so, I felt resentful and scared of the widening gap between my-parents-as-they-were and my-parents-as-they-are.

二
十
三

TWENTY-THREE

I thought more and more of Chuin-mei. I wanted so much to see her, but whenever I considered actually walking down the path, I was much too scared.

At the end of the second week in October, a few days after Dad's release, I went to the kitchen for a jug of water. The cook was standing at the stove putting pieces of unrefined sugar in a pot. He took a long wooden spoon and stirred the sugar to prevent scorching, and murmured rhythmically, "She is here. She is here. She is here."

I watched him for a few minutes with my hand on a white enamel jug. This is probably the only sure chance to see Chuin-mei, I thought. I knew the cook's wife was uncomfortable when I visited, but now he seemed to be encouraging it. What could it mean? My decision swung back and forth: should I or shouldn't I?

Benjamin burst in, startling me so that I knocked the jug to the floor. "What's the matter with you?" he asked. "You look as if you swallowed something."

"Nothing," I mumbled, and stooped over the jug to hide my confusion.

"Sometimes you act like you've gone bonkers. Where's Mum?"

"I don't know," I said through clenched teeth.

180

Benjamin ran outside.

Briefly the cook left his stirring and did something with the flour scattered on the table where he had been kneading bread. Then he went back to stirring and murmuring, "She is here. She is here."

I picked up the jug slowly, started toward the water crock, and saw what the cook had done with the flour. My face burned. I gazed for a long minute at his back, then made up my mind. He had drawn Chuin-mei's and my symbol of friendship. I put the jug back on the shelf and went out toward the small house, glancing about to make sure Benjamin was gone. I knocked, but nobody answered. I pushed the door open, but no one was inside. My heart pounded. "Chuin-mei?" I called in a frightened whisper.

"Here I am," Chuin-mei answered in a whisper from behind the bedroom curtain. I went in. "My aunt is at the market with the baby," she hurriedly explained from where she sat on the large family bed. "I've been here several times. Why haven't you come?"

"Why are you in here?" I asked, growing more scared because of the air of secrecy that was suddenly surrounding everything.

Chuin-mei twisted her braid around her right finger. "You didn't come before, so I thought it would be better to meet where we are not easily seen."

"What did you tell the cook?"

"He is loyal to you," Chuin-mei said, answering my unasked question. "You will never know how loyal. Still, I knew it was a risk, but I saw no other way. Why haven't you come?"

I looked uncomfortably at my hands and picked the

edges of a wart. I was deeply ashamed of my suspicions when she was willing to risk this much for me. The police checks were so much more frequent these days that the chance of her being found here with me was much greater and could mean trouble. "I almost didn't come this time," I told her. "But you must have shown the cook our character and told him to use it."

"I did. I knew you would remember."

Hearing the warmth in her voice, I looked up. "When I saw it, I couldn't *not* come. My mother—she said I wasn't to see you anymore. I wanted to tell you, but there's been no chance." I looked pleadingly at Chuin-mei. "They are both scared, especially since my father was in jail."

Chuin-mei looked away. "Parents!" she said enigmatically.

"Your father holds you back, too?" I asked.

"There are things my father wants me to do that I cannot do," she said in an undertone.

"So you haven't—so you weren't—so you didn't agree with my dad's arrest?"

She touched my shoulder as if I was a child. "I, too, am loyal," she said passionately.

I was even more ashamed. I couldn't think what to say. I knew now that the complications she faced were far greater than I had dreamed. "I wish you could come with us to Hong Kong whenever that happens," I suggested longingly. As I looked at her, I realized this would probably be the last time we saw each other. "It would be so much easier to talk without—"

"No," Chuin-mei interrupted. "You must go. There's

no place for you in our revolution. But I have much to do."

In my overexcited mood, her words sounded cool, impersonal, like a stone being slung at me. "Is it . . . is it dangerous?" I managed to ask.

A slight smile crossed Chuin-mei's face as she tossed back her braid. "Sometimes it is dangerous. But I look where I walk and my feet are steady."

"You're brave!"

"*You* can work for revolution in *your* country when you get there," Chuin-mei suggested eagerly.

"Me!"

"Yes. Do they have revolutions in America?"

"Well, that's how the country started," I said slowly.

"You see! Revolution is good. It brings in the new ways. Maybe I will come to help you one day. I have learned the English."

"You . . . mean that?" I asked. So this was why she wanted to learn English, I thought—to come to America and help bring about a revolution!

"Yes! Yes! Truly I mean it!" she answered.

I watched her in confusion: this was something I hadn't even considered. "I suppose I won't see you again. Maybe I should go back."

"It would be interesting to see America," Chuin-mei said shyly. "Let us stay friends." She stood up and we put our arms around each other.

Suddenly we heard men's voices in the outer room. A dark hand clutched the edge of the curtain and pulled it back. Dad stood there behind the policeman with the thick glasses, the one who made the most frequent inspections. Chuin-mei pushed me aside and stood straight, facing the man. I hung back. My heart pounded and my knees wobbled so much that I was afraid I might fall.

A fly buzzed past and settled on the officer's collar. He raised his hand to brush it off, then lowered his arm. The movement showed a brown mole on his neck. He looked straight at Chuin-mei with a hard, impenetrable expression. "What is my daughter doing in our relatives' house—relatives who cook for Westerners?" he sneered.

Chuin-mei flinched, as if this was something she hadn't expected. But she answered without hesitation. "The cook's wife is at the market. I am waiting for her return."

"Tell the wife of the cook that she is expected at the accusation meeting tonight."

"I will tell her," Chuin-mei said.

"Your turn will come," he told her in a horrible hard voice. Then he turned to me. "Why are *you* in the house of the cook?"

My mouth was so dry I could hardly get out the words. "I'm . . . I'm learning embroidery," I stuttered. "I forgot my work today, but . . ." My voice dried up.

The policeman sneered, did an about-face, and left to join the others outside.

"Get to the house," Dad said, ignoring Chuin-mei, his voice low and harsh.

I ran past him and up the back stairs. I threw myself on my bed, pulled the pillow over my face, and held it there with both hands. The confusion of my thoughts sharpened into a burning anger, but against what? Against whom?

Suddenly the pillow was yanked off. "Sit up!" Dad ordered. "Explain yourself."

184

Slowly I sat up and leaned forward in a sullen slouch. "You won't understand," I said slowly and deliberately, knowing I was hurting him but unable to control myself.

"No," Dad said. "I certainly won't. Your mother told you never to visit that girl again."

I pushed my hair off my hot cheeks and went on staring at the floor. "Dad, you're wrong about her. You don't trust me. You're wrong. She's my friend. A real friend," I cried out, becoming more convinced, as I said the words, that I was right. "She wouldn't do anything like you think. I know it." To myself I thought: There must be really deep disagreement with that horrible father of hers. It was *not* like Dad thought, it wasn't some sort of awful plan.

But then Dad was quiet so long that my skin began to prickle with fear. "I hope you're right," he said at last in a dull voice, and walked heavily from the room. I felt as if I'd slapped his face. I picked up the pillow and threw it as hard as I could at the floor.

二
十
四

TWENTY-FOUR

I almost wished Dad had whipped me, or made me write pages of apology, or assigned some hateful task—something, anything, to clear the fog bank of my parents' disapproval. But nothing happened. After their initial questioning, which focused mainly on Chuin-mei's political opinions and my responses, Mum and Dad seemed to ignore me. Time dragged like an illness.

On the afternoon of the third day, I went out to milk the cow as usual. Automatically I checked the rope that tied her to the tree, then stood for a while with my hand on her smooth tan back. The consolation an animal brings soothed me a little. The cow's tail whisked my arm and I pulled up the stool, then realized I'd forgotten the bucket from the kitchen. I got back up.

Mr. Hilary, who had come silently acrosss the grass, was standing beside me. "Ruth, what's happened?" he asked.

The unusual kindness in his voice took me by surprise; most of the time he was so matter-of-fact. My eyes filled with tears. "Sorry. I don't mean to cry. Everything's so horrid. I think I might have made things dangerous for my father and my friend. And I wonder . . ." I hesitated, afraid to say the next words, though I'd thought them

186

often enough in the last few days. "I almost wonder if I've invented the friendship. I wanted it so much. But all she cares about is the revolution," I blurted out.

"You've certainly taken a risk. Your father told me a fair bit about it."

"Dad doesn't believe me. He doesn't trust me. He doesn't know Chuin-mei at all!" I cried out.

"What experience have you had with politics, Ruth? Now think."

"Politics?" I asked. "I haven't had any."

"Have you any idea of the government pressure to make Westerners look guilty? You remember what I told you, how people are encouraged to find a specific act or opinion for which to imprison Westerners or send them from the country in disgrace?"

"Yes," I said, and let my eyes rest on a leaf which had fallen on the cow's back.

"What makes you think you can safely manage where so many are stopped by the uncertainty and dangers of the revolution?"

"I thought you admired everything Chinese!" I exclaimed in disbelief.

"I had supposed you were getting chiefly one-sided Western opinions," he explained. "I might not have expressed myself quite so strongly if I had realized you were hearing the Chinese point of view. But there are dangers to them as well as to us. Anyone who finds she's been with you could use it against her."

I glanced up briefly. Something moved on the other side of the pomelo tree. "Chuin-mei knows the revolution is dangerous, but she's so clear and courageous about it all!" I choked on my words. "I think everything's such

187

a huge, complicated problem, but it's so straightforward to her."

Mr. Hilary thought for a few minutes. "I don't know Chuin-mei," he said carefully, "but she sounds to me like an ardent revolutionary who has heard the propaganda and swallowed it." He sighed. "There's a certain value in it. She'll learn the problems soon enough."

"But she's not like that! Hating America is part of the propaganda and she's friends with me. It's not some kind of treachery like all of you seem to think!" I picked up the oval leaf from the cow's back and tore off bit after bit. "I like her so much. And I just want to be friends," I finished under my breath. I watched the leaf fragments flutter to the ground, then glanced up, since Mr. Hilary said nothing. I expected some sort of reasoned argument against what I'd done. Instead, there was a look of pained sympathy on his face which astonished me.

"Do you remember the friend I told you about—?"

"Catherine? The one who gave you the Wordsworth book?"

"Yes. We went with some others on a walking holiday one summer in the Lake District in the northwest of England. One of the things we discussed was the disciplined aspects of friendship."

"I don't think I understand," I said.

"Friendship has its pleasant, comfortable aspects; but sometimes, to remain a true friend, you have to be so generous you're willing to give up the friendship for the sake of your friend. You remember the Bible story of David and Jonathan."

I nodded, wondering what had gone on between him

188

and Catherine, but knowing it would be impertinent to ask.

"Jonathan has always seemed to me an extraordinarily generous man: sending his friend away to keep him safe, asking nothing from him."

I nodded again and rubbed the tears off my face.

"Right now your friendship with Chuin-mei is dangerous for her as well as for you. Your father said Chuin-mei's father seemed very perturbed when he found his daughter with you. There's no telling what he may do. Family members are actively encouraged to accuse each other."

I began to cry again.

"It's never easy. Little of worth in life is easy," Mr. Hilary said. He came closer and put his hands on my shoulders.

My cheeks burned—he had never touched me before. I was dismayed by the thoughts that burst into my mind. I wished he'd put his arms around me, hold me close. I'm crazy! I thought. He'll notice. He'll think I'm silly. I curled my toes inside my shoes, and stood rigid with embarrassment. Then I swallowed to control my voice. "I forgot the bucket," I mumbled.

He took his hands from my shoulders. "I'll fetch it," he said gently, and left. The kitchen door slammed behind him.

I felt his hands on my shoulders like flames. A snort of laughter came from the upstairs veranda, and I lifted my head and squinted. Through the branches of the tree I could see three pairs of shoes poking between the vertical rails, and three heads above the horizontal rail. They were watching, I thought. They saw us! I turned even hotter with vexation and bit my tongue.

"We saw Mr. Hilary hug you!" Benjamin sang out.

"You beast!" I snarled, and ran into the house, scrambled through the luggage room and onto the porch, with no clear idea in mind.

Benjamin stood on the middle of the bench, where the others still sat. "We saw Mr. Hilary hug you!" he sang out again, and gave Trevor a cheeky wink as if pleased with the excitement he was creating.

"You—you—" I lunged at Benjamin. He jumped down and dodged. I caught his shirttail, and Simeon and Trevor laughed. Even Simeon! I thought in a wounded rage. We've had arguments, but he's never mocked me. I grabbed for my youngest brother's arm and he ducked and lurched hard against the rail. It was loose and swayed out with a screech of wrenching wood. He fell through and landed clumsily in front of Mr. Hilary, then crumpled without a sound.

Mr. Hilary dropped the milkpail, knelt beside Benjamin, and lifted his limp hand. The rest of us stood by the broken rail, horrified. "Is he dead?" Trevor asked in a hoarse whisper.

Mr. Hilary put two fingers on Benjamin's pulse. "He's fainted," he said at last, "and it looks as if his leg's broken. Find a pillow and blanket and fetch your father."

I didn't move. My eyes were fixed on Benjamin.

"Did you hear me?" Simeon asked.

I nodded. "What did you say?"

"You get the blanket," Simeon told me. "I'll get Dad. Come on, Trev."

I stumbled like a sleepwalker through the luggage room

and to the blanket closet. For a couple of minutes I stared at the shelves, then slowly took down a tan blanket and went back outside.

By the time I reached the group, Mum was leaning over Benjamin, stroking his damp hair and trying to console him. She had given him a wooden spoon to clench against the pain. He must hurt terribly, I thought as I watched his white knuckles and listened to his choked moans.

"I'll go to the police station for permission to get him to the hospital," Dad said, turning to the bicycle shed. "See what you can do to make a stretcher, David."

"Ruth," Mr. Hilary ordered me, "find all the large safety pins you can, and bring them here. I'll get poles and another blanket." I went after him, grateful to be given something more to do.

When we had collected everything, we spread the second blanket flat, laid the poles on it, and pinned the sides of the blanket securely to each other around them. Together we lifted the makeshift stretcher next to Benjamin. He was in too much pain even to be curious. He seemed unaware of anything or anyone except Mum. "Is he coming yet?" he kept moaning. Mr. Hilary went to the gate once more to scan the street.

Trevor stood on the grass behind Simeon, watching fearfully.

I hovered near the stretcher, hardly able to take my eyes off Benjamin's white, contorted face or to block out his moans. I glanced up and caught Simeon looking sympathetically at me and was deeply grateful.

At last Dad came back with the necessary papers, which he placed on the blanket, then put away his bike. Very carefully he and Mum lifted Benjamin onto the improvised stretcher. Benjamin screamed and fainted again. Tears rolled down Trevor's dirty face, making clean streaks.

Dad and Mr. Hilary picked up the stretcher and went through the gate. "I'm sorry you can't come, Lillian. Pray," Dad said to her. We watched the two of them trot rhythmically down the street, heading for the hospital three miles away.

Simeon walked with me up to our room. I dropped on to my bed and buried my face in my arms. "Why don't you leave me alone," I said in a muffled voice.

"What's been going on?" Simeon asked gently.

I moved one arm a little and waited. Might as well let him know, I decided. He can hardly think worse of me than he already does. So, in a dull drone, I told him about my last visit with Chuin-mei. "Now, why don't you say I'm terrible as well?" I ended.

"I don't think you are," he said quietly.

I lay absolutely still, not sure I'd heard him right. Then I looked up at him. "But you warned me!"

"That was easy enough. She wasn't *my* friend."

I dropped my head again. "Oh, Sim."

二
十
五

TWENTY-FIVE

My parents didn't punish me. I think they saw I was punishing myself quite enough. I tried to be as helpful as possible, although my preoccupation with all the woe I had brought made me very forgetful. Simeon was kindness itself in his own understated way, often acting as a buffer when he saw I needed him.

A week after the accident, Benjamin was back from the hospital and thoroughly enjoying his new importance. On the veranda outside the dining room, he reclined royally against his wicker sofa. It was a Grecian-style sofa with only half a back, one curved arm, and six slender legs. Trevor perched beside him on a stool, folding paper airplanes for him to toss.

"Ruth, get me a drink," Benjamin commanded me.

I stood at the window, dustcloth in hand, letting the scene with Chuin-mei churn through my mind. Mr. Hilary's comment about her father haunted me. Had I tangled her in more danger?

"Hurry up, Ruth," Benjamin said. I had heard him, but only on the fringes of my consciousness.

"Okay, Benjamin," I said, glad enough to have him order me about since it seemed to be the only way to make up for what I had done. He was certainly happy to take advantage of it.

I was back a minute later. "Anything else?"

"Yes, um, Ruth, find me something nice to eat. Oh, and some for Trev." They snickered as I left.

I brought out a blue-and-white rice-pattern bowl with a couple of figs and some peanuts in it. The two of them counted and announced their total, 26 peanuts. "Anything else?" I asked.

"Yes. Let's see." Benjamin looked around. "Get my Chinese checkers."

I brought a low table and set the game on it. "Is that all?"

"No," he said. "Find Simeon, and both of you play with us."

For a while the only sound was the quiet tick of the marbles in the tin tray. "Come on, yellow," Benjamin exclaimed impatiently. "You go. Wake up, Ruth. You're yellow."

"Lay off, Benjamin. Leave her alone," Simeon said.

I slid him a grateful look.

Mr. Hilary came by. I slouched lower on my stool. He tapped the cumbersome cast and said, "It looks as if we can start school tomorrow. We'll arrange ourselves out here with you."

"But I'm sick!" Benjamin protested. "I can't do school when I'm sick."

"It's only us four left now," Trevor added accusingly.

"We can start school tomorrow," Mr. Hilary repeated.

I stared down at the yellow marble I had just moved, hoping he would leave soon. I knew he was puzzled by my behavior—each time he had tried to talk to me alone,

I had evaded him. But I couldn't explain, and only made mumbled excuses. Since his other efforts had failed, he had given me extra assignments, which he must have thought would hold my interest. "Have you finished working out the cast of characters and their relationships?" he asked me.

I was so afraid of what Benjamin or Trevor might say that I couldn't think clearly. "Which?" I asked.

"For *War and Peace*. I suggested it a couple of days ago," he added.

"No, not exactly," I answered.

"It is complicated, but I wouldn't have thought it was so difficult," he said. "Would you like me to help you?"

Benjamin and Trevor giggled. "Shut up, Benjamin Thompson," Simeon growled. "And you, too, Trevor Clark."

"When will you—" Mr. Hilary began.

"I don't know. I have to . . ." I jumped up and ran into the house, my face hot with confusion.

"Is she sick?" I heard Mr. Hilary ask.

"Stomachache," Simeon answered, covering for me.

Mr. Hilary's footsteps went on.

I washed my face so hard I felt I was scrubbing the skin off, then combed my hair, got a drink of water, and went back out. Benajamin looked up and opened his mouth to make some comment, but I stared him down.

Several turns later, Miss Hilary walked through the door. "Let's have your stool, Trevor," she said in her comfortable gravelly voice. "You've probably wondered what was in my purse. Children always do." She undid the clasp and several tiny beads ticked onto the Chinese checkers board. "I always keep a few toys for emergencies." She dug around in her purse and laid things on top of the game: a couple of letters, a New Testament in Chinese, a black fountain pen. "Ah! Wonderful! Splendid! Here we are." She held up a miniature ivory dominoes game and a small flip book. She zipped the pages for Benjamin: a stick figure acrobat did his exercises while a black dog ran back and forth.

"Thank you!" Benjamin said, and grinned into her face.

She gave him an affectionate smile.

Dad strode through the door, triumphantly waving several passports. "You're on your way!"

"Who? Who?" we asked.

"As usual, it's their own assortment," Dad said. "You, Martha, Lillian, Simeon, and Benjamin."

"Isn't Ruth going? And Trev? And you, Daddy?" Benjamin asked.

Dad frowned. "Did I forget to say Ruth? Yes, you're going, too," he said to me.

"What about Trev?" Benjamin persisted. "And what about you, Daddy? And when are we going?"

"Trevor and his parents are going to help me with some final business, eh, Trevor?" He patted the top of the little boy's head. "You go tomorrow morning," he added, and left us.

Trevor scowled and got up. "I'm going to find my mum."

"Trev!" Benjamin cried out. But he ran inside. Benjamin stared after him.

In a little while Miss Hilary said, "You'll have to find some good places for Trevor to visit when he gets to Hong Kong."

"Like what?" Benjamin asked without interest. He zipped the pages of his little flip book back and forth, idly watching the pictures move.

"There are lovely beaches, and ferry boats to various islands, and a funicular railway, and—"

"What's a funicular railway?" Simeon asked.

"It's a railway that goes up the side of a mountain, with two counterbalanced cable cars."

"I bet he'd like that, don't you?" Simeon asked Benjamin.

Benjamin frowned as if he was thinking through the possibilities she had listed. "Yes," he said. "I think he'd like the funny railway."

That night I lay in the dark and imagined wearing the new dress Mum had found and saved out of one of the trunks. The fabric was forest green, sprigged with silvery green leaves and flowers. By some miracle it fit properly, making me look like a queen, Benjamin had told me admiringly, with its hooked bodice, three-quarter-length sleeves, and full skirt. In a narrow linen envelope that had been packed with it was a Honiton lace collar designed in primroses. "Your great-grandmother did work like this," Mum had told me as she held up the intricate lace and smiled through it. "She was from a family of lacemakers. I used to love to watch her with her lace pillow in her lap, working her little bobbins so fast you wondered how she kept from tangling them." She chuckled. "Each bobbin had a wire ring of beads to weight it. She named the bobbins, depending on where she got the beads, I think: Nancy, Ethel, Serena, Ursula."

Then I thought of Dad's words, letting them echo in

my mind—they were like a welcome for the new Ruth to a new life. "I've got the bus tickets," he had told me. "You'll have to get the boat and train tickets on the way."

It was only then that I realized they must have found a guarantor. "But you, Dad, when will you get out?" I asked.

"I pray, soon." And then the words, "Take care of your mother for me."

"You trust me!"

He had looked up with a warm smile. "Of course I trust you."

I had stood silent in front of his desk, letting those words penetrate the anguish of the past days, letting them give me the courage to ask what I had to ask. "Do you think . . ." I started, and quailed. "Do you think, before you leave, you could ask the cook about Chuin-mei?" I clenched my fists until my nails dug into my palms—I didn't want to spoil what he had just said to me.

"I'll see what I can do," he said tonelessly, the smile gone from his face.

二
十
六

TWENTY-SIX

After several false starts, we finally got underway on the last day of October. At the bus station, I submitted, in a kind of daze, to being inoculated and to being frisked. I kept my eyes fixed on the bus: a big shuddering vehicle which reminded me of those large yellow school buses I had seen in America a few years before.

"Your luggage!" a soldier shouted from the roof of the bus, where he was tying suitcases, baskets and bundles. "Give it to me."

I stood on tiptoe, pushed my case up the side of the bus, and moved back. Then I thought with grief of Chuin-mei. Where was she? What was going to happen to her? Was her father really out to get her, or did he simply want to scare her into submission?

Mr. Hilary stood nearby with his sister. "It's almost time to hoist you in," he told Benjamin, then turned to me and put out his hand. I thought of his gift: *War and Peace*. On the flyleaf he had written: "For Ruth from David Hilary. October 1951. We find little in a book but what we put there. But in great books, the mind finds room to put many things.—Joubert, 1842."

Even with a big dollop of sentimental imagination, there was no way his Joubert quotation could be romantically interpreted. I put my hand in his and smiled into his face. "Goodbye, Mr. Hilary. Thank you for teaching us," I said stiffly.

"I'd have been a desolate man without that interest to sustain me." He gave my hand a firm farewell clasp. "Never stop reading."

"I won't," I assured him. "Goodbye." His face blurred, and I turned my head.

He moved on to Simeon. "Goodbye, Simeon. Send me some of your drawings when I'm back in England."

"Be happy to, sir," Simeon said.

"So long, Benjamin, my friend. Take good care of that great cast of yours."

"I'm going to. It weighs nineteen and a half pounds. I weighed it the other day. Trevor helped me." He fished around in a blue cotton bag tied to one crutch, pulled out his miniature dominoes set, and gave it to Mr. Hilary. "I was going to keep it, but Trevor needs it more," he said, looking up woefully.

"I'll give it to him," Mr. Hilary said, and pocketed the little box.

Dad, who had been taking care of some final details, strode up to the group. "We're all set," he told us cheerfully.

Hugs. Kisses. Tears.

"Come soon, Dad," Simeon growled.

Briefly Dad took both of Simeon's hands. "Remember, Simeon, you're the man of the family going downriver." We all chuckled.

"Take care of yourselves," Mum said to the two men.

"We'll be praying for you," Dad answered.

"Goodbye."

"Bye."

With a great clamor of voices, sheetmetal, horn, and gears, the bus pitched down the narrow street: past the little houses, past curious children, past the police station, past the propaganda posters, through the city gate, and out onto the packed dirt road leading southeast. That evening we reached an inn at a village on the Yangtze River where we had to wait for several days.

One morning, when the soldier who guarded us took us to the dining room, Mum gasped and looked delighted. We were allowed to talk only to each other and usually said nothing, fearful that the simplest thing would be misinterpreted by the soldiers. Mum sat down, obviously trying to control her excitement. Furtively, I looked around. Then a woman seated alone near a window began to talk into her rice bowl. "I was freed from jail by the kindness of the People's Republic of China," she informed her bowl. "My protectors are ushering me to the bridge to Hong Kong. They treat me with great courtesy."

"That was Miss St. Claire," Mum told us when the soldiers had locked us back in our room.

"Do you suppose she's been in jail all this time?" I asked, horrified.

Mum nodded. "They must be deporting her, but she looks as if they treated her somewhat reasonably."

Two weeks later we were able to get boat tickets for the next part of our journey out of the country. Deck space was all we could buy.

The following morning Simeon and I were leaning on the rail of the river steamer. "Boy, am I glad we're out of that inn!" Simeon said. "Two weeks shut in that hot little room with Benjamin is enough to frazzle even Mum. I'm glad we have several days of this."

We looked across the deck to where Benjamin lay, still asleep, with an old man and several soldiers crowded next to him. On his other side, Mum and Miss Hilary sat on the deck, leaning against a vent, watching the spectacular Yangtze Gorges slide by. The cliffs were so steep the sun shone on the churning water only at noontime.

"I wish Dad could have come with us," Simeon commented, "or I could have stayed with Dad."

I stared down at the frothy water. "Well, I'm glad you're with us," I answered after a while. "I can't imagine what it'd be like if you weren't around." I glanced affectionately at him, grateful that our old easy relationship had come back. "Do you ever wonder what it'd be like to live in a place where things didn't happen all the time?"

Simeon stared up at the narrow rope tower's path cut into the vertical cliffs. "It's hard to imagine not being a missionary's kid."

"Do you really agree with Mum and Dad?" I asked.

"About what?"

"Going to foreign countries and being missionaries."

"Well, yes," he answered.

"Sometimes I don't," I said more emphatically than I'd intended. Simeon looked startled. "I guess . . ." I went on, fumbling with my thoughts, "I guess they have to follow their consciences."

"What do you mean?" he asked.

"It would be easier if they didn't, but I'd respect them less. Sometimes I wish they'd chosen an easier life. In England or America, maybe."

202

"Then they wouldn't have met each other and we wouldn't be here," Simeon said promptly.

"Oh, Sim." I laughed. "You're so practical."

Late on the afternoon of the second day, the steamer passed into the wide, slow, yellow water beyond the Gorges. It stopped for the night, then sailed on for two more days. In the evening, we landed, were frisked again and packed onto a train.

"Ayah. Ayah," Mum groaned when we'd squashed into our seats.

"What?" I asked.

"That!" She glanced up at the loudspeaker hooked to the corner of the railway carriage.

"Mao Tse-tung, Si-ta-lin . . ." it blared forth, day and night.

At every station, every passenger got out and was frisked; suitcases were emptied and inspected. Each time, Simeon watched anxiously, hoping they wouldn't take his singing emperor. Each time, Benjamin was careful to point out his cast. At the end of the fourth day on the train, at one of the last inspections we would have to undergo, Mum asked me to keep an eye on Benjamin while she and Miss Hilary went to find the privy. He sat on the platform with his chipped and grimy cast stretched out in front of him. He had pushed back the cotton padding so often it had grown stiff and gray with dirt. He cupped his hands around something and peeked in every now and then as if to make sure the thing was still there.

"What's in your hands?" I asked.

"Something that bites," he said, and his eyes sparkled.

"That bites?" I repeated with amused suspicion.

A soldier with a heavy limp elbowed his way through the passengers and stood over him. "Open!" Benjamin held open his hands and looked up. "I must confiscate these," the man said. On that little scamp's dirty palms lay a set of false teeth. The soldier leaned over, picked up the teeth, examined them carefully, and put them in his pocket.

I was aghast. "How did you dare!" I didn't know what the soldier might think of them, but concealing anything alarmed me.

Airily Benjamin explained, "Police and soldiers usually like me."

"They do seem to." I couldn't help but agree as I watched the soldier make his way eagerly toward a group of friends, gesticulating at his pocket and his mouth as he approached. "Wherever did you get false teeth?"

"Out of one of those trunks."

"What trunk?" I asked, watching the delighted interest of the soldier's friends.

"In the luggage room."

"Oh." I turned back to my young brother. "Where have you been carrying them?"

"In my cast."

"Do you have anything else in there?" I asked quickly.

"No."

"Are you sure?"

"Well," he said slowly. "My leg."

The train rattled, roared, and hissed, and propaganda blared, until at last we reached the final station on the mainland border of the British Crown Colony of Hong Kong. People poured from every opening. Our party and a few others joined the inching column onto the little footbridge which crossed the gulley marking the border. It was a small, casually constructed bridge, with the planks laid more or less evenly across the supporting beams.

Benjamin craned out of line, frowning. "I thought that was the Bridge to Freedom."

"It is, but you must be quiet until we get across," Mum told him.

"But it's such a crummy little bridge. You could kick those planks off. It looks like something I built."

"Sssh," Mum cautioned.

"But look at those poles at the sides," he kept on in a hoarse whisper. "They look like they're meant for beans to climb up, not sides of the Bridge to Freedom!" He was quiet a minute, and we all breathed more freely. "And that umbrella tied to the pole by the policeman," he hissed, pointing with his finger held close to his cheek. "It's more like for a scarecrow in the bean patch!"

"Benjamin!" Mum exclaimed anxiously. "Don't even whisper those things!" She frowned, casting about for something to distract him. "Think about the ice cream we're going to look for."

"What's that?" he asked.

"That special dessert I told you about."

I glanced over my shoulder at the fluttering Communist flag with its golden hammer and sickle. Clusters of soldiers were standing here and there. I wonder if Chuin-mei and the rest of the people will survive this revolution, I thought. But then I imagined what Mr. Hilary's answer might be. "Survive? Certainly they'll survive. They're Chinese. They've always survived. I see no reason to suppose they won't manage this time, too!"

205

Something brightly colored, flapping on the other side of the bridge, caught my attention. I squinted at it. Briefly, it spread out in the welcome breeze. The Union Jack! Suddenly the dream seemed real, the dream of being an ordinary Western person in an ordinary place doing ordinary things.

Just then, two bright-eyed Chinese soldiers hollered at Mum and Miss Hilary, who moved closer. The men twitched the papers from their hands and scrutinized them minutely, reading out the words and glancing at each other, occasionally discussing something. One part seemed to annoy them. They spoke among themselves, quietly at first and then more loudly, while we grew more and more anxious. Finally the soldiers nodded in unison. "Go!" they ordered, and pushed the papers toward us, then stood cracking their knuckles, watching as we stepped onto the bridge.

We walked carefully across without saying a word. But when we were firmly on the free side, all of us, even Simeon, shouted.

"Hooray!"

"Thank God!"

"At last!"

A thin, bent man wearing a suit four sizes too big who had crossed just ahead of us joined our group. A slow, incredulous smile spread over his face. We all hugged each other and then we all burst into tears.

"Why are we crying?" Benjamin asked.

"For joy," Mum said.

The British soldier standing beside the flagpole smiled, as if this was the way everyone who crossed that bridge behaved.

二十七

TWENTY-SEVEN

A week after we arrived at the refugee center on Hong Kong island, Trevor and his parents joined us. "Now we can go on the funny railway," Benjamin told his friend. "I hope it's sunny so we can see all over."

"Is it high?" Trevor asked.

"Terribly high," Benjamin explained. "At least, I think so. I haven't been on it yet. I was waiting for you."

The day after the excursion, Miss Hilary sailed for England and her very old parents. Two and a half weeks passed with no news at all. We prayed for Dad and Mr. Hilary but didn't speak of the fear that was at the front of all our minds. On the sixth day of the third week, the two men arrived. It was like crossing the bridge all over again.

Mr. Hilary went to stay with an army friend at a barracks on the mainland. Dad told us about the day they got their release. "A message came to the mission home for David and me to go immediately to the police station," Dad said. "They questioned us for an hour or so, and then one of the policemen said we could go home. They'd never phrased it quite like that, so I asked, 'Home to Paper Lantern Street, or home to our countries?' 'Your countries,' he snapped."

I was dying to ask Dad about Chuin-mei, but didn't dare. I kept hoping he would say something. That evening, a little before sunset, he took me outside to a bench under a maidenhair tree. "I know you want to hear about your friend," he said, "but I wanted to wait until we could talk quietly."

I watched his face for some clue. He was frowning as usual, but not deeply. He did look very weary. I shifted forward to the edge of the bench. "Did you find out what happened?" I asked nervously.

"A couple of days after you left, there was another of those terrible accusation meetings in the yard, and Chuin-mei's father was one of the accusers."

I swallowed; it was the very thing I had dreaded. "What did he say?"

"He worded his accusations," Dad went on, "as though she had been disloyal to the party. He said Chuin-mei had talked secretly with an American imperialist spy— that was you. But after some of his ranting I had the impression he was thwarted in something he wanted her to do." He stared down at his hands cupped over his knees.

The sun appeared from behind a cloud, making the whole Hong Kong harbor a golden sea.

"At first," Dad continued, "I wasn't sure what he was getting at. But then he explained himself more specifically. I think he was trying to forestall having his daughter make counter-accusations. By the end of the whole business, I was so impressed with her decency and self-control . . ." Dad paused and shook his head without finishing the sentence.

I held my breath. Dad's news was more than my wildest hope could have led to. "What was he trying to get her to do?"

A yellow leaf fluttered from a branch of the tree and dropped to the bench between us.

"There was a list of things," Dad said. "But then he told the crowd he had urged her to confess the American's plot and that she had refused. He must have been thwarted in other ways, that time the two of you were at the cook's. It's a nasty business, this setting family members on each other." He stared out over the harbor, where a fleet of six fishing boats was just setting out. He sighed and then smiled. "When Chuin-mei was asked for her counter-accusation, she said simply that she had tried to carry out his instructions but you were too young and too uninstructed and too stupid to be useful."

I smiled, thinking of some of our conversations in which Chuin-mei knew exactly what she thought, and I merely fumbled my way through.

"There must have been another meeting somewhere else where further accusations were made, because she disappeared for a couple of weeks and I feared the worst, because the cook knew nothing. But when I went to the police station to pick up our exit visas, she had been assigned to give them to me. It was obvious she had been through some ordeal, she was so ill at ease and had such dark rings under her eyes, but I don't know what had happened. What clinched her innocence in my mind was that when she brought in the exit papers she handed me something and whispered, 'For Ruth.' I was mighty scared for her, I can tell you. If anyone had seen her, I don't know what the consequences would have been."

"I think she enjoys risks," I said.

He sighed. "She must."

"Did you know that that man was her father?" I asked. "Before that day at the cook's?"

"No, I didn't," he said, and put his hand into his inside jacket pocket.

"Does Mum know?" I asked.

Dad nodded.

"Did she say anything?"

He smiled. "You know your mother, always ready to excuse everyone except herself. She didn't blame either of you." He brought out a long cream envelope with a scarlet border, which he gave me.

My hands shook as I pulled out the thin sheet of paper, tattered at the edges. "It must have been inspected a lot," I commented.

"Oh, yes, but there's nothing to criticize in it," Dad said. "Chuin-mei certainly has her wits about her."

Very carefully, I opened the letter. At the top was an exquisite paper cut of a red persimmon and several leaves; and underneath, very carefully written: "From your friend always." Dad read the characters for me.

"I think you were right, Ruth," he said. I glanced up. "She really is your friend." He smiled, but with a sadness that puzzled me.

I gazed at the words and shivered as I thought of the risks she had taken for the sake of our friendship. How could I have been so uncertain? That love for her new government, which I thought was first and foremost with her, she kept in a perspective I hadn't understood. She honored her father in her way, she was friends with me, and neither of those things was approved by the new government. We had both been heedless of the consequences, or else had ignored them, I wasn't sure which. All at once I understood Dad's sadness: my friendship had added to Chuin-mei's danger in ways I'd never know. It was on the tip of my tongue to ask what would happen to her. With a sickening awareness, I realized Dad couldn't answer. Probably I'd never know.

On December 21, 1951, arrangements for our departure were completed. From the stern of the large American ocean liner, our family and Trevor's watched as sailors shouted and loosened ropes, and the pilot boat busily moved into position.

"Did you know we're going to live next door to each other?" Benjamin asked Trevor.

"Where's your place?" Trevor asked.

"Chicago, Illinois, United States of America, and my Aunt Ruth and my Cousin Jane and some other relatives and things are there. Where's yours?"

"Brantford, Ontario, Dominion of Canada, and my Granny and Grandpa Clark's there and some cousins and things."

They smirked at each other, then exchanged a few friendly punches.

Simeon and I stood side by side, leaning against the rail, staring down at the wake of the ship which stretched all the way back to shore. "We'll probably never see China again," I said.

"I don't really care what we do, as long as we can stay with Mum and Dad," Simeon said in deep contentment.

"You and I have been a lot of places together," I went on lazily.

" 'Wayfarers all,' " Sim answered.

"That's for sure. How many thousands of miles?" I asked, not really expecting an answer. I pictured a globe with our travels marked in a jagged red line, the way trade routes are marked: West China to India to East China to England to America to central China to West China to East China. And now west again to America. A new life, I thought, starting all over. It was frightening. And exciting.

The extravagantly beautiful Hong Kong harbor glided farther and farther away. All the crowding and poverty along the shore blurred into a picturesque patchwork of rooftops. The low blue hills grew smaller and smaller, until at last they sank into the deep blue water of the South China Sea.

FIC
VAN

Vander Els, Betty

Leaving point

$12.95

DATE			
OCT 1 6